YULETIDE SPACE RANGER

A SPACE PIRATE CHRISTMAS STORY

C.G. HARRIS

Hot Chocolate Press

The Viraquin Voyage series is a 4-book space pirate adventure.
Think Guardians of the Galaxy meets Firefly

The Viraquin Voyage Completed Series:

Hometown Space Pirate

Stowaway Star Runner

Yuletide Space Ranger

Space Pirate Reunion

<u>QR code for Free Novella, Fugitive Star Voyage,</u>
to read the origin story for this series.

Join the C.G. Harris Legion

Join the C.G. Harris Legion to receive book intel, useless trivia, special giveaways, plus you'll learn about Hula Harry and get his Drink of the Week.
https://www.cgharris.net/legion-sign-up-page

ONE

"What do you mean that's it?" I stared at the main display screen located at the front of the bridge. It occupied the majority of the forward space in stark contrast to the icy blue curves of the ship's hull. "How can that be the planet Santa comes from? That looks like Megatron's version of the Deathstar."

We had spent weeks traveling the galaxy to visit an alien species touted to be the origin of the modern-day Santa Claus. We needed information, and their propensity for spreading Christmas cheer made them uniquely suited to provide it. The hard part would be convincing them to give it to us.

Lois, my first mate, walked up next to me and stared at the screen as well. She wore bright yellow combat boots that matched a bomber style jacket. Her lipstick was as red as her glasses, and she wore her long blond hair in a ponytail. I stood six-four with dark hair, dark T-shirt and jacket, and formed an imposing presence, but at four foot nine, Lois could back down a grizzly bear when she wanted to.

"Eight tiny reindeer could never live in a place like that," she said. "I don't see a spec of land anywhere. There isn't even any snow. How can Santa and his reindeer live in a place with no snow?"

"As usual, your mix of modern culture and erroneous folklore is astounding." The voice was Buttercup's, our not so artificial intelligent ship's computer and navigational system. She was a live consciousness that had been uploaded into the mainframe. An illegal and unethical practice, but one that had preserved her life, and now we reaped all the cynical benefits. She had a numeric designation, BT3RCP, but I had named her Buttercup soon after we met. She hated it and I made sure to use it every chance I got.

"The sleigh and reindeer originated from an unfortunate accident witnessed in the early eighteen hundreds. During a Christmas deployment, the assigned *Santa* was forced into an emergency situation. A coordinated attempt to facilitate his capture. He managed to escape but had to utilize a rather unusual form of transport to get back on schedule again."

"He used a sleigh and eight reindeer?" My eyebrow shot up in disbelief. "Did he have something against using a horse?"

"There were no horses, nor were there any reindeer." Buttercup amended. "The witness, Clément Clarke Moore, took a great deal of poetic license when he later wrote a poem about the experience. The sleigh was actually a broken-down dog sled and the only animals available to pull it were a pen full of goats."

"Wait." I held up a hand. "You're telling me the first Santa rode a sled pulled by eight mangy goats?"

"Not quite the poetic impact, I must admit," Buttercup continued. "He was not the first Santa, but yes, he utilized the tools at hand and managed a heroic escape."

"Wow." Lois peered over her glasses at the sine wave

Buttercup overlaid on the screen, a visual representation of her speech. "Sort of takes some of the magic out of the story."

"Believe me, there is still much magic to behold. The technological advances of the Dazbog, whom you refer to as Santa, are legendary. Your little human brains will be sufficiently blown."

I walked to the front of the bridge to my captain's chair and spun it to face me. There were three chairs situated in a triangle pattern with the captain's position slightly forward of the other two. The current occupant looked up at me and gurgled with glee. She was the whole reason we were here.

Our resident baby Viraquin was a bioluminescent wonder few had ever beheld. She had a smooth domed head and short little tentacles that wriggled more than walked. Her big, blue doe eyes could melt the heart of any monster, and she had a cute little mouth that seemed to perpetually produce bubbles, thus her name, Bubbles. She was soft and pink, except for the bioluminescent blue light that pulsed under her skin, and the smallest splash of freckles that stood in place of a nose. A plush toy company would make millions producing anything half as cute and Bubbles.

No one, to our knowledge, had ever seen, much less had contact with, a baby Viraquin. They were incredibly rare in any form and possessed a unique power coveted by almost every intelligent creature in the universe. Bubbles could fold space. She had the ability to move herself and everything around her to any point in the universe in the blink of an eye. It was an incredible power and one to which there was no defense. She could pop in behind enemy lines and pop out without anyone being the wiser. The perfect guerilla warfare weapon.

Unfortunately for us, Bubbles was a baby and babies know

not what they do. As far as she knew, folding space was nothing more than a fun little game. The trip to Santa Planet had taken weeks longer than it should have because of Bubbles' occasional space folding detours. We would get close to our destination, then Bubbles would get bored or think of some other place she wanted to be and zap, we were light years away. It was a frustrating exercise, and we could not figure out what made Bubbles decide to fold. As far as we knew, it was nothing more than a whim.

"Let's try to stay on course this time," I said, eyeing Bubbles as she rocked back and forth in my chair. "No zapping or folding or throwing us into uncharted space. You hear me young lady?"

Bubbles gurgled a little laugh.

"I don't think she's taking you seriously," Lois said. "I'm telling you. There should be consequences for her actions. She's powerful. Bubbles needs to know that using her power whenever she wants to is *not* okay."

I shook my head. "She's a baby. How are you going to punish a baby? Put her in time out? She'll just fold somewhere else. She doesn't even understand what she's doing."

"That's the point." Lois glared at me. "It's our job to teach her, at least until we can get her back to her mother."

That was our true mission. To find Bubbles' mother and return her to where she belonged. Unfortunately, the Viraquin were all but a myth, so finding her home proved difficult to say the least. The Dazbog, or Santas, traveled further than most species due to the unique nature of their mission. We were here hoping they could tell us where to start looking.

"Well, she's not folding now so I think we're good." I turned toward the screen and tried to ignore Lois as she crossed her arms and narrowed her eyes. "Let's get down to that metal monster and see if we can get some answers."

"It may be prudent to hold at the Dazbog's outer boundary and hail them from here."

"Why?" I scoffed. "It's Santa Planet. If there's a more friendly place in the universe, I can't imagine where it would be."

I spun my chair forward again and leaned on the back. As I did, Twitch, our Chitterwall, became visible and scurried up to my shoulder to make himself at home.

He resembled a cross between a flying squirrel and a red and blue macaw. He had beautiful plumage when he chose to remain visible, but when he didn't, he could change his colors like a chameleon and blend into any background. He was smart as a whip, an incredible thief, and best of all, he always agreed with me.

"What do you think, Twitch? Should we swing down and say hello?"

I held my fist up to him and he returned the gesture with his tiny hand.

"See, Twitch agrees. Let's go visit Santa and tell him what we want for Christmas."

"To be clear," Buttercup said. "They're not Santas, they are the Dazbog. I suggest you refer to them as such unless you wish to resort to your usual tactic of pissing them off as soon as you meet them. And it is not 'Santa Planet,' it is Daedala, an organized, efficient and mechanized planet devoted to one thing."

"Let me guess." I grinned. "Making toys."

Buttercup sighed. "Yes. I can see this is going to go quite well. Lois, perhaps you should take the lead in contact and negotiations this time."

"Hey."

"I couldn't do any worse than you." Lois laughed.

I shot her a glare but couldn't argue. When it came to first contact, I was about as diplomatic as Yosemite Sam.

"Let's just get down to *Santa Planet*," I enunciated the name to be extra annoying. "And go from there."

"As you wish."

I turned to the viewscreen and saw that we were moving again. There was no physical perception of movement inside the ship thanks to the inertia dampeners, but I could see the planet getting bigger as we approached.

"Maybe we should listen to Buttercup." Lois stared at the screen as well, but a glance out of the corner of my eye revealed a nervous looking furrow in her brow. "She knows more about etiquette than we do. Maybe we should hail them first and get permission to approach."

I scoffed. "It'll be fine. It's not like we're rushing into a battle zone with guns blazing. We're just stopping by to say hello."

"Yeah, but you still knock on the door before you walk into the house."

I hadn't thought of it that way. Maybe they were right. I was about to tell Buttercup to send out a friendly hello when alarms began to shriek over the speakers and the border around the screen turned red.

"We have triggered the planetary defense system." Buttercup's voice sounded somewhere between panic, and I told you so. "We have multiple missile locks. They are preparing to fire."

TWO

Lois stared at me. Bubbles stared at me. Twitch stared at me. I was pretty sure if Buttercup had eyes, she would be staring at me too.

"All right, so I was wrong. We ran into a little problem. Are we going to dwell on it or deal with the issue at hand?"

"A problem you caused." Lois amended.

"With your permission, I will attempt to open a channel to Dazbog command."

"Hold on a sec. What are we going to tell—"

"Permission granted." Buttercup cut me off before I could finish my sentence and I heard the tell-tale static of a spotty connection crackle over the speakers.

"You are in restricted space. Turn back or be destroyed." It was a voice transmission only, but I recognized the gruff tone. It reminded me of a Dazbog we met on Fafnir space station in the Shedu system. He worked as a bartender at the Black Star, but he turned out to be much more than a humble barkeep. Stella pulled our bacon out of the fire more than once and if I ever saw him again, I would owe him at least as many rounds as he could drink. I considered him a friend, and friends like that were hard to find.

"We're not here to cause any trouble. We just want to speak to someone. We were sent—"

"You are in restricted space. Turn back or be destroyed."

I looked at Lois. It was the exact same phrase as before, but I wasn't sure it was an automated response. Lois shrugged, offering no help at all.

"We were sent by the Peeri to speak to you about—"

"I don't care who sent you, where you are from, or why you are here. You are in restricted space. Turn back or be destroyed."

That time I knew it was a real Dazbog we spoke to.

"Look, we don't want to cause any trouble, but we've come a long way to speak to you. Is there any way we can land and talk with someone? We don't even have to leave the ship. You can send a San— Dazbog out to meet us." I caught myself short of saying Santa and Lois shook her head in disbelief.

I ignored her skepticism and raised her a cocked eyebrow, proud of my diplomatic problem-solving prowess. She rolled her eyes and pinched the bridge of her nose with her fingers. I'm pretty sure she was impressed.

There was no response from the Dazbog. I waited for a moment, hoping our less than gracious host would agree, or at least come to a compromise, but we were met with nothing but dead air.

"Did they hang up?"

"This is an interstellar communication system," Buttercup said. "You do not, *hang up*."

"You know what I mean. Did they cut off the transmission? Are they still there?"

"The channel is still open, but it appears they have chosen to end negotiations."

"Now what?" Lois threw her arms out in exasperation. "Do we just sit here?"

"I would not suggest that course of action. The Dazbog still have a lock on our position. They might fire on us at any moment, though I have to admit, this seems aggressive even for them. Security can be stringent due to the proprietary nature of their mission, but I have never encountered outright aggression."

I stared at the sine wave annotating Buttercup's voice.

"You've had contact with the Dazbog before and you didn't say something earlier? Why didn't you warn me about their security ... whatever?"

"I believe I advised you not to approach the planet and suggested you hail them, but you were quite sure Santa Claus was giddy with excitement to hear all your Christmas wishes."

I grumbled under my breath. "You know if you're going to spend all your time ridiculing everything I say, you can just take me back to Earth and find someone else to captain your ship."

Lois snorted out a laugh and was about to add her two cents to the conversation when the viewscreen flashed on in an explosion of light. It took my eyes a second to adjust, but when they did, I saw a Dazbog face staring back at me.

I realized too late that Bubbles faced the screen, and I cursed as I spun her backward out of view. Our goal was to keep Bubbles as safe and secret as possible but somehow, we (as in me) always managed to expose her to every alien we ran into.

"What did you say?" The Dazbog on the screen didn't so much as glance at Bubbles. His eyes were focused on Lois and me. So much so that I felt a little uncomfortable.

"I was talking to Buttercup, our ship. She's always joking around about —"

"Not that, you clueless vistic. You said you were from Earth."

"Yeaaaah." I drew out the word not quite knowing how else to react. "Is that a good thing?"

The Dazbog narrowed his eyes, scrutinizing our faces.

"Step away from the screen so I can see you better." He barked the order so loud, Lois and I obeyed before I could even think to question it.

"Well, I'll be. Humans. Who would have thought a couple of humans would show up at my doorstep to help at a time like this."

"Excuse me?" I raised a finger. "To help what? We're only here for some information. We aren't planning to stay long. Just a quick visit. You'll hardly know we were here."

"Permission to approach." The Dazbog ignored my protest. "Follow the coordinates sent to you, and do not deviate or you will be destroyed."

The transmission cut off, and this time I could tell it was more than the silent treatment.

"What did he mean by help?" Lois looked at me.

I shrugged. "I have no idea."

"Given our circumstances," Buttercup added. "I believe we have no other choice but to proceed to the planet and find out. We've been supplied with strict coordinates to a docking area. If we deviate or attempt to retreat, they will fire."

I blinked. "Well, that isn't quite the welcome I hoped for, but at least we've got our foot in the door."

"Yeah." Lois shot me a sidelong glance. "But what are we there to talk about? Something tells me they're not allowing us to land because they want a friendly chat over tea."

"It's only polite to hear what they have to say." I tried to appear convincing as I smiled at her. "Nothing says we have to agree to help them. I'm sure they're reasonable. We'll have a friendly conversation, explain that we're on an important mission, get our information and then leave."

I turned to look at the screen, watching the ominous looking planet grow larger as we approached. Just chat and leave. I'm sure that'll be no problem at all.

THREE

It didn't take long for us to make our way to the coordinates the Dazbog provided. As we approached and flew over the planet, we received a bird's eye view of the metal titan. The closer we got, the more frightening the place became. From space it resembled a huge ball of ragged steel, but now we could see the outer workings begin to take shape.

There were superstructures, warehouses, and manufacturing facilities as far as the eye could see. There were no discernible residential areas, just industrial goliaths pumping steam out of red and white striped smokestacks. Everything was connected, and the whole planet seemed to churn like the inner workings of an intricate clock. We were too high to get a good look, but there was an interweaving road or walkway system too. Buttercup set down on a stark metal pad jutting out from one of the factory buildings. The moment we did, I saw a welcome party rushing forward to greet us.

"How is the atmosphere here?" I asked, as we zipped our coats and I eased my backpack into position. I adjusted the straps on the banana yellow hard-shell container and clipped the waist belt. Inside the assault hardened pack rode our infant Viraquin. We had learned the hard way that leaving her in the ship only resulted in her folding to wherever I happened to be standing, usually at the most inopportune times. Buttercup fashioned this transport container so Bubbles could see out but no one else could see in. I was amazed by the innovative material she had used, but Buttercup considered it no more advanced than a piece of carry-on luggage. I only cared that it would keep Bubbles safe and hidden from any prying eyes that might seek to steal her away.

"The atmosphere on Daedala is conducive to human anatomy." Buttercup reported. "However, they do have a high level of contaminants in the air."

"What do you mean by contaminants?" Lois held up a hand, presumably to hold Buttercup from opening the outer door.

"I believe your people refer to it as *smog*." Buttercup drew the word out as if it left a bad taste in her mouth. "The airborne contaminant level is high, but no higher than many of the cities on Earth. Though, on Earth pollution of this level carries a much heavier toll due to the natural state of the planet, not that humans care."

I wanted to snap back with some sort of denial, but Buttercup was right. If humanity excelled at one thing, it was ignoring the ugly problems that mattered the most.

"I would feel a lot better if I could bring my revolver." I patted my right hip where my space revolver usually hung on expeditions like this. It was a sci-fi giddy-inducing piece of tech full of lights and power. It approximated an old west revolver, but turning the cylinder changed the firing sequence to anything from stun to tank buster.

"Considering the level of security outside, bringing a

weapon of any kind would be unwise. In your case I would even shy away from paperclips and cotton balls."

Lois snorted out a laugh. "Yeah, please don't attack any of the guards or do something that will get me killed. Or if you do decide to do something stupid, at least give me time to move out of the way."

Twitch glided in and landed on my shoulder then stood on his hind legs, using my head for balance.

"I can be diplomatic." I huffed. "By the time we leave, I will have these guys eating out of the palm of my hand."

Lois groaned.

I glanced at Twitch who was preparing himself for the ride in with us.

"It might be best if you sit this one out. We want to minimize the number of visitors as much as we can."

Twitch chittered and motioned toward the pack on my back as if to say, why does Bubbles get to go and he can't.

"Come on." I pleaded. "You know we can't leave her here. I promise, next time we head out to meet some new aliens you can come with us."

Twitch chittered again, then jumped into the air and glided away to a stack of crates and disappeared in a fade of pouting camouflage.

I looked at Lois who stared at me with a sardonic expression.

"What? He's sensitive. I just want everyone to be happy."

Lois shook her head, but I ignored it as I stood next to her on the exit ramp. "Okay, I think we're ready. Go ahead and open the door."

Buttercup complied and the door opened in a rush of hissing steam. I squinted though the vapor, trying to see outside as we descended the gangplank looking for our welcome party.

"Hello? We're here to meet with ..."

It occurred to me that our host never gave us his name.

"We were invited to speak with someone about some information we're—"

I was cut off by six figures rushing to surround us. They were not human. They weren't even Dazbog. The figures were strange looking automatons scurrying around on four little spider legs that clicked and clacked on the metal decking.

Their arachnid legs carried a top half that was ... well they weren't quite humanoid so much as human shaped. They were short, maybe four feet tall and they had gleaming green mechanical arms and cylindrical torsos. A set of blocky white designators printed on the front, like a high school football jersey, differentiated one from another. The one to my right was LF 14, while the one to my left read LF 39C. They all had different designations, but every one of them began with LF.

Their head was the most alarming feature of all. Each of them grinned at us with the face of a smiling cherub. Not a life-like moving representation, but a static, smiling mask in the same green color as the rest of the body, finishing off the polished monochromatic scheme. The only thing that didn't bear the forest green color of their shell were the designators and the gleaming white lights that shone as eyes in their pudgy little faces. A delegation of decayed Kewpie dolls would be less creepy, but they were apparently here to escort us to our host.

"Are you serious right now?" Lois had her arms pulled in tight to her body as if she were afraid one of them might reach out and grab her. "I'm not going anywhere with these things."

I shot her a tight-lipped grin. "Diplomacy, remember? I thought I was supposed to be the problem child."

"That was before we were attacked by robot babies."

"Come on, they're not attacking us." I tried to keep my

smile, but I began to feel the sweat prickle my forehead. "Remember that adage about judging a book by its cover? I'm sure these are very nice robot babies. Who ever heard of an evil baby?"

"Have you ever seen *Chucky*?"

"Chucky wasn't a bab— never mind. I'm going in to get this over with. You can stay with Buttercup if you want to."

I saw the conflict in Lois' eyes, but after a second she relaxed her arms and steeled her spine. "No, I'll go with you. But if one of these things touches me ..."

I snickered. "Maybe one of them will hold your hand."

The automatons somehow comprehended we were ready to go and began to walk. Their spider legs clicked and clacked in an uncoordinated chatter as we walked. The sound was almost as unnerving as their appearance. They didn't carry any weapons that I could see, but something told me they were more than just a pretty face. All I wanted to do was meet our host, get the information and leave, but the farther we walked with our infant entourage, the less likely that seemed.

Despite my uncertainty, I could not help but marvel at the industrial automation that whirred, hissed and clanged all around us. The walkways I had seen from the air weren't walkways at all, but conveyor belts that carried all manner of parts, items, and much to my inner delight, wrapped gifts and finished toys.

The buildings, landing pad, actual walkways, even the sky appeared to be constructed from of the same steel gray that consumed the entire planet. There were no adornments other than the occasional red and white striped smokestacks. No neon lights, no billboards, houses or suburban yards. Everything was built for one thing and one thing only. Production. I could hear, smell and taste the oily metallic atmosphere of manufacture and assembly. No one ever envisioned the North Pole looking like this.

We walked through a set of automatic doors and entered the towering building attached to the landing pad where Buttercup was parked. Inside the halls looked much less industrial. I wouldn't call it homey, but there were tiles on the floor and the walls were made of something that resembled drywall or plaster rather than steel. It could have passed for a quasi-government building on Earth except for one thing. There were no office workers within the office. In fact, the one conspicuous thing that seemed to be missing everywhere on the planet were the Dazbog. Even if it was not their custom to escort guests into the building, I expected to see a few of them wandering the area. If we were on Earth, you couldn't walk around without bumping into a human. This was just another in a long list of details that made me think we were not going to get out of here as easily as we hoped.

At the end of the hall stood two sliding glass doors. The LFs led us through, and inside I saw something I did not expect … again.

This planet was supposed to be dedicated to the production and distribution of toys. The room we stood in had huge screens along the walls, rows of computers manned by more of the LF units and one large desk that oversaw it all. This was not an operations center for a toy factory, this was a war room, and the Dazbog controlling it marched toward us as if we had just kicked in the doors to his secret sanctum.

FOUR

"What took you so long?" The gruff-looking Dazbog marched toward us so fast part of me wondered if he might attack. "Do you have any idea how valuable my time is? Do you understand what I'm orchestrating here?"

I leaned back as he stopped way inside my personal space.

The Dazbog were what humans would identify as a satyr. Half man, half goat. But that wasn't the real surprise. The fur on their legs was not brown but fire engine red. They had coal black hooves, long white beards, and a Dazbog we met on the Tennin space station even wore little round glasses and smoked a corn cob pipe. Add a big red coat and a hat to cover the horns, and the iconic Santa figure was unmistakable.

This Dazbog, however, wore no shirt and smelled somewhat of barn sweat. He still had a distinctive resemblance to Santa Claus ... if you covered the hairy chest and horns, but there was no cheery smile or jolly disposition.

"I'm sorry." I took a full step backward and extended my hand in a gesture of greeting. "I think we may have gotten off on the wrong foot. I'm Ben and this is Lois." I gestured in her direction, and she nodded, offering her best smile.

"I'm General Peloren Kreasha. Most know me as General Pen."

"Forgive us for asking," Lois looked around the room taking in the rows of computer banks, LF units and huge wall screen monitors. "But what is it that you're doing here? Where are all the other Dazbog?"

"We're at war." General Pen threw out his arms and turned from us, moving a few steps toward the main floor. "Isn't it obvious? I'm commanding our off-world troops, but the threat is advancing and I'm not sure it can be stopped. That's why I brought you here."

"Brought us here?" I held up a hand. "We just came for some information. Directions really. We're looking for—"

General Pen turned to face me, cutting me off before I could finish. "The Dazbog are forbidden from revealing state secrets."

I stood with my mouth half open not knowing what to say next.

"So, what is this threat?" Lois said, taking up the conversation.

"Threat? It's only a threat to the very evolution that shapes our universe." General Pen stepped forward, closing the distance between us. "The Dazbog are charged with tending that galactic garden, and if we can't preserve Christmas, the fruit that nourishes its expansion will wither and die. And your planet is first in line."

I blinked.

"Are we in the middle of a save Christmas story?" I grinned. "I love Christmas movies. Which one is your favorite? I love *A Christmas Carol*. The original, not all the terrible remakes. I mean Christmas is not really in trouble in that story, but Scrooge is definitely—"

"Ben!" Lois backhanded me in the stomach, and I realized General Pen was glaring at me. Perhaps Christmas movies were not his thing.

"This is not a laughing matter. What we do is too complicated for your tiny human brains to ever comprehend. I should have never brought you here. Get out."

General Pen began to walk away but Lois hurried after him, no doubt seeing our only chance to get the information we needed slipping though our fingers. "Wait. We're sorry. Can you please explain? You brought us here for a reason. At least let us know what it is."

General Pen hesitated and turned to face us again, his face pinched with frustration. "If I wasn't so desperate ..."

"Good," I said hurrying next to Lois. "Thank you. Please tell us about this whole Christmas problem. Are you saying you created Christmas?"

The implications of that question didn't hit me until the words were out of my mouth and I found myself wishing I hadn't asked in the first place.

"Of course not."

I let out a breath I didn't realize I was holding and heard Lois do the same.

"We did, however, create Santa Claus."

FIVE

I let out an uncomfortable chuckle, then realized I was the only one laughing.

The smile fell from my face, and I raised an eyebrow instead. "What do you mean you invented Santa Claus?"

"Do you think it a coincidence that a mythical children's character on Earth happens to look like a Dazbog?"

It did seem like a bit of a stretch. A big stretch in fact. It was one thing for people to pass down ancient alien sightings and have them melt into myths, stories and folklore. It was another to have one that influences modern society.

"Okay, let's say for a second we believe you. Why would you create such a character? Do you just want a reason to spy on us once a year?"

General Pen rolled his eyes and turned, beckoning us to follow him. Lois and I complied, keeping pace with the odd gait of the satyr.

He stopped at the nearest workstation and the LF unit scurried away on its spidery mechanical legs. I peered at the creepy cherub face and shivered, not quite turning my back on it.

"What's the deal with these robot things? Why did you make them look like that?"

General Pen glanced at the perma-grinned LF unit. "We are tasked with a massive production cycle. Much more than any biological workforce could handle. The LF units, or Labor Force units, are the backbone of our construction and assembly team. We work with such a large population of these units that a member of our senior staff thought it might be helpful to make them more relatable. The face was an attempt to make them appear more ... alive I suppose. We fired the developer, but the faces were such an undertaking to integrate we didn't have the time or resources to undo the disaster, so we just got used to them."

Lois snickered as General Pen turned toward the workstation and busied himself pulling something up on the screen. I looked at her and raised my eyebrows in question.

"Don't you get it." She leaned toward me and whispered. "LF units. Ellfff." She drew out the pronunciation of the designator phonetically. "They're elves." She snickered again as the realization sunk in and I shook my head. This was all getting to be too much.

General Pen stepped aside so we could see what he had pulled up on the screen. It was a video loop of Earth and the unending issues that plagued humanity: pollution, war, famine, fossil fuels. It showed all the bad and none of the good, and I felt a not-so-subtle pang of defensiveness rising into my throat.

He glanced at me. "Before you get all high and mighty about love and the creativity of the human condition, let me say we are on your side. But this is reality. Your planet is being consumed by all manner of neglect and destruction and you're not alone. Many fledgling civilizations suffer the same fate. It's always a race between the base instincts of greed and power, and the evolution of enlightenment that allows a civilization to transcend and live in harmony with their environment. Sometimes this race has a clear winner on one side or the other, but sometimes that race is a little closer, and that's where we come in."

General Pen swiped his hand across the screen and the image changed from the disastrous image of Earth to a basic illustration of a human child holding a toy.

"What we do is lend a hand to species that might otherwise lose the race to self-destruction. All it takes is a little evolutionary push and ..."

He touched the screen again and a cartoon wave emitted from the toy toward the child's head.

"Presto, humanity evolves into a species smart enough to outrun its own self-destruction."

I blinked at the screen in horror and disbelief. "Are you telling me you're radiating children with your toys?"

"No, of course not ... well yes, sort of. Allow me to explain. Our toys are embedded with proprietary technology called the Micro Magnetic Pulse Emitter. This emitter can be programmed to target the area of the brain known to trigger ascension to the next evolutionary phase of life. Stimulating this area during childhood triggers minute changes that are then passed on to their children, generation after generation."

"How long have you been doing this?" Lois looked as shocked as I was. "On Earth I mean."

"We have done it for countless centuries, refining our technique throughout the ages, but we've only been operating on Earth since your year of 1820."

"What?" I took a step backward, unable to resist raising my

voice. "You've been zapping kids on Earth since the eighteen hundreds? That means I've been zapped. Lois, you were too."

She grimaced.

General Pen's lip curled up in a sneer. "Careful. Your presence here, as well as this little instructional sidebar, is due only to my good nature. I would not suggest getting on the wrong side of it."

Lois held out a hand in front of me to stop any further accusations. "Of course. We're sorry. This is all a lot to take in. So, you're helping humans evolve faster than normal?"

General Pen nodded and then glared at me. "Good thing you brought someone with some intelligence along."

I bit my lip and nodded without replying.

"Every generation is a little smarter than the last," Pen continued. "Furthering problem solving and solutions to what would otherwise be your downfall."

"Fascinating." Lois nodded "Those all sound like good things. I don't see the downside."

"There was no downside, as long as we delivered our Emitters on time. We had even begun adding enzymes to our packaging and ribbons that would help decompose some of the more harmful plastics that plague your planet."

"Why do I feel like there is a big but coming?"

General Pen eyed me again, but after a moment he relented with a nod. "The Emitters do have a weakness. Due to their near microscopic size, their power cells are limited to a little over one of your earth years. If we don't return to renew the supply of toys each year, the Micro Magnetic Pulse Emitters will cease to operate. If that happens ..."

"Then what?" I prompted.

"An infant in the early stages of treatment will regress to

their normal state, but any child in later stages of treatment, what you call toddlers to adolescents, would not survive."

"What?" Lois and I shouted at once.

"Are you saying all the kids on Earth might die?" I couldn't help but take a step toward him. Messing with our physiology was one thing, killing kids was in a whole other stratosphere.

"You must understand." General Pen held up his hand to forestall our fury. "The alternative was the likely self-destruction for your entire race. We've carried out this mission for centuries on countless other planets without a single catastrophic failure. We would not fail now if it were not for the Cur who have turned against us and wish to destroy all we care for."

"Wait," I said. "What ... or who, are the Cur?"

As if on cue, every screen in the room flashed with a red warning banner and alarm claxons went off all over the facility. The LF units began working at a feverish pace, but General Pen just stared at us, hardening his resolve.

"Stay here much longer and you might have the misfortune of finding out."

SIX

General Pen turned toward his desk at the front of the room, raising his voice as he walked so we could hear him over the growing noise made by the LF units.

"I don't have any time left for explanations, either you are willing to help or you're not. I don't have the energy to debate any longer."

"Wait." I shouted and looked at Lois. "I still don't understand who, or what, the Cur is ..."

I trailed off as General Pen walked away, obviously unwilling to continue the conversation.

"I believe I can assist you in that regard," Buttercup said over our internal communicators. "The Cur have worked with the Dazbog for centuries, providing an item required to achieve the otherwise impossible task of delivering gifts to every child in the world in one night. It is known as the Void Prism, and it has the ability to split an individual into countless versions of themselves. This allows one Santa to be in a vast number of locations at once. Without it, the Dazbog's mission would be impossible."

I hurried forward, catching General Pen as he got to his desk. "So, this Void Prism. Are you fresh out or does the Cur provide them one at a time? How does it work?"

General Pen looked at us, surprise registering on his face. It didn't last long though. Within half a heartbeat he began typing away at a keyboard and working something on a touchscreen we couldn't see.

"The Void Prism is not your problem, at least not in the way you mean. The reason we are running out of time, and that no Dazbog are here, is because we must keep the Cur away from this planet. If they advance close enough to use their Void Prisms, we will be overwhelmed, and the war will be lost. It would only take one ship to break through our lines and ..."

General Pen didn't seem to want to finish the statement, choosing instead to growl in angry frustration.

"So, what is it you want us to do?" Lois threw out the question before I could stop her.

We had already put ourselves in so much danger on these side missions I was not eager to do it again. Still, this wasn't any old space problem. This was Earth. We couldn't turn a blind eye on our home when we might be able to make a difference.

"Forward support was supposed to send a transport ship for the deployment to Earth. The ship must have been destroyed or they simply couldn't spare one for the trip. I deployed the supply fleet under a cloaking field weeks ago, but we need our trooper to go in and complete the mission."

"Are you saying you want us to bring Santa to Earth for Christmas?" I could not help but laugh out loud. I looked at Lois and she had a grin on her face as well. I felt an odd mix of anger, fear and childish excitement at the prospect.

"This is no pleasure cruise." General Pen jumped out of his seat and pounded his fists on the desk. "Every Cur in the quadrant from here to Earth will be gunning for you. They will do anything to stop you from reaching your destination. The only thing you have going for you is that you are not flying a Dazbog ship, but it won't be long before they get wise to that. As soon as they see your trajectory, they'll shoot you down."

That was enough to wipe the smile from my face. Were we really going to do this? Was Buttercup going to become Santa's proverbial sleigh and put us all in danger of dying ... again.

I was about to open my mouth to say something when General Pen turned his head and nodded toward two new visitors. They had not come through the throng of working LF units, but rather from a passageway on the side I hadn't noticed before.

Both of the new arrivals were Dazbog. They each wore black tactical vests as a sort of uniform, but that's where their similarities to one another ended. One personified a perfect physical specimen of a Dazbog. If he were human, he would be Chris Hemsworth on his very best day as Thor. Muscles rippled across every inch of his body and his face was chiseled into a perfect square, even under his long white beard. I thought it would take quite a bit of padding over those ripped abs to make this Santa plump and jolly.

While the first Dazbog marched in toting nothing but his testosterone fueled pecs, the second lagged behind. He was small and meek, carrying a backpack far too big for him to control. His reedy legs looked as if they might buckle under the pressure if he had to carry the load much farther. The little Dazbog had the trademark white beard, but his grew more like scraggly weeds than full lustrous hair.

"This is Dirk. Our most decorated trooper." General Penn nodded toward the mountain of muscle. "He will accompany you on your mission. He has completed numerous deployments, several of them to Earth, which is by far the most dangerous."

I wasn't sure whether to greet Dirk or question why Earth was so dangerous. I decided on the former.

"Nice to meet you. And who is your companion?"

Dirk turned, looking over the other Dazbog's head at first, then looked down as if surprised to see him.

"Oh, there you are," Dirk said in a low and commanding voice. "I was wondering if you would make it."

"This is Elliot." General Pen said the name as if he described spoiled meat. "Dirk's apprentice. I suppose he'll need to accompany you as well."

"Good to meet you too, Elliot." Lois and I shook their hands.

Dirk had a firm grip and winning smile, while Elliot spent more time leaning forward to balance his backpack to avoid toppling over.

"These humans offered to transport you to your deployment."

I saw Dirk's smile falter. "Excuse me sir? Can I have a word with you—"

General Pen cut him off with a wave. "All the usual transports were either destroyed or deployed to the resistance. These humans were selfless enough to offer their services without any thought of recompense."

I cleared my throat. "Actually, there is one thing."

General Pen shifted his glare to me as I ruined his pretentious dialogue.

"I told you, the Dazbog do not—"

I held up a hand stopping him from finishing. "I know, I know, but the least you can do is listen to my proposal."

General Pen crossed his arms but didn't say anything else

and I took that as an invitation to continue. I looked at Lois, then nodded my head toward my pack. I had been wearing it the whole time, but Bubbles had been blissfully quiet, refraining, for once, from calling any attention to herself.

Lois nodded her head in approval, and I shrugged out of the pack, swinging it around so I could settle it onto General Pen's desk.

Revealing Bubbles was not only inevitable, but necessary. Our passengers would learn about her on the ship and there was no way of asking for my information from General Pen without telling him about her. At least this way maybe Bubbles could melt his heart with those big blue eyes of hers.

I opened the top and without any explanation, retrieved an adorable baby Viraquin out of the pack.

I had no doubt that the Dazbog were accustomed to seeing some surprising things, but this set even them back in a gasp.

"This is Bubbles," I said. "She has been left in our care, but we'd like very much to return her to her mother. The information we seek is not for our gain or to gain us any advantage or wealth. All we want to know is how to get her home. In your vast travels, if you happen to know where the Viraquin might live or hide we would appreciate the information. Not for us, but for Bubbles, so that she might see her mother again."

Bubbles looked at General Pen as if scripted to do so. She hit him with those big blue eyes just like I hoped, and the surly general melted like butter.

"All right," he sighed. "Considering the circumstances and your selfless motives, I will provide the information."

I smiled and glanced at Lois. She clapped her hands and grinned with excitement as well.

"But only after ..." He paused on that last part for effect. "You have completed your successful mission to Earth."

My spirits sank a little at the word successful, but at least we had a deal.

"I do have one question," Lois said, raising a finger. "What about the Void Prism? Won't they need that to complete their mission?"

I couldn't help but grin at the fact that she had taken up their military vernacular concerning Santa's mission on Christmas.

General Pen nodded. "Unfortunately, there is nothing you can do about that. I have deployed several covert missions in an attempt to attain a Void Prism. If they're successful, the recovery team will meet you at the deployment site."

"If I may." For the first time, Elliot raised his hand and spoke up. His voice was much more soprano than the other two and he spoke with less volume. "It's possible that I could have a solut—"

"We do not have time for your ideas and gadgets," General Pen said, cutting him off. "Stay focused on your mission and try to learn something from Dirk."

Elliot lowered his hand and nodded. I felt a little sorry for him, but there wasn't much I could say. I didn't want to sully the deal, and besides, we would have plenty of time to talk on the ship.

"All right then." I pulled Bubbles into my arms out of protective instinct and smiled. "I guess we have our mission. All we need to do is avoid the Cur, get to Earth in one piece, and hope we can deliver about a billion presents in one night."

SEVEN

I gave Dirk and Elliot the ten-cent tour of the ship, then brought them to the bridge. They had met Lois and Bubbles, but there were still a couple of introductions to make if they were going to be traveling with us for any length of time.

"I'm afraid we only have three seats up here. Buttercup should be able to fabricate a fourth, but until then we'll be playing musical chairs." I walked to my captain's position and shrugged out of my carrier pack.

Bubbles had been inside for quite a while, and I was sure she would be eager to get out. I pretended not to notice when a telltale light flashed out of the pack, followed by a soft pop that buffeted my ears. A millisecond, and one more ear buffeting pop later, Bubbles landed in my chair.

I glared at her with a scolding eye. My seat faced forward so the others hadn't seen what had transpired, but a quick glance at Lois told me she had felt Bubbles fold as well. Maybe she was right. If we didn't get this thing under control soon, Bubbles might find herself in real trouble one of these days. For that matter we all could.

Lois gave me a hard look, then sat in her seat leaving the third chair vacant. Dirk wasted no time claiming that position as his own.

"Who's Buttercup? Is that the name of your maintenance droid? I've never heard of anything but an LF unit who can build items upon request." Dirk scanned the bridge as if he expected a robot to come rolling out of the glassy blue walls carrying a hammer and nails.

"Buttercup is the third member of our crew. The ship's sentient computer and navigation system. She's a bio-intelligence and our very good friend, so if you have a problem with having her on board you are free to leave right now."

It was a little heavy handed, but a live consciousness stored within a ship's computing system was not just illegal, it was considered immoral. In the short time that we've been together, she has been called an abomination more times than I wanted to count, so I thought I had a right to be a little over-protective.

I met Dirk's eyes and waited for a reaction. He stared at me for a moment, his mouth half open as if he were about to say something unwise, then his lips widened into a gleaming grin, and he shook his head. "A bit less than traditional, but as far as I understand, you're our last hope for completing the Earth mission on time. If we have to bend a few rules to get there, who am I to say no?"

Elliot snorted out a laugh from behind us and I turned to look at him. He had taken off his gargantuan backpack and was now digging deep inside.

"Something you want to say?"

"Take it easy, Ben." Lois tried to stop me from pressing any further, but I wanted everything out in the open before we got started. I held up a finger to her but kept my eyes on Elliot. He seemed unconcerned and continued rummaging in his pack as he spoke.

"I have no problem with Buttercup, great name by the way, I just thought it was funny that Dirk said he was willing to bend a few rules. He usually gets all twitchy if you wrinkle the rule book at all."

Elliot seemed to find what he was looking for and withdrew a thin metal rod from his pack. He held it out like a cane then butted it against the floor and it unfurled, reverse umbrella style, into a stool big enough for him to sit on. Seemingly satisfied with the accommodations, he took his seat and leaned against his pack looking every bit as comfortable and we did in our chairs.

"Rules are put in place for a reason," Dirk snapped. He tried to sound casual and unconcerned, but it was more than a little obvious that Elliot was deep under his skin. "Bend the rule, break the back of society, that's what I always say."

"That's a little black and white." Lois smiled at him. "But I understand how important it is to set and abide by rules."

I glanced down at Bubbles who made herself comfortable in my chair. "Or to break them." I added.

Elliot snorted out a little laugh and I knew who I would favor on this trip.

"Buttercup, can you work on fashioning a fourth seat here with the others? I would like it if we all had a place here together."

"Of course." Buttercup broke her silence for the first time. "It will take a few hours, but I can construct one behind your captain's position."

"Thanks." I smiled at the forward display screen where her sine wave lit up, annotating her speech. Due to a unique molecular control over her hull, Buttercup could construct just about anything given the proper time, materials and available power. It wasn't instant, but it was still pretty amazing.

A nondescript bump began to rise out of the floor behind my chair and I did my best not to stare as it grew into a gradual lump of self-molding material.

Elliot made no bones about staring at the activity while Dirk turned away in what looked like revulsion. Yup, definitely going to pick favorites.

"With your permission, I have been given the coordinates to an exit corridor," Buttercup said, redirecting everyone's attention to the forward screen again. "I suggest we get underway as soon as possible. We have a long trip ahead of us and if General Pen was right, we may have to detour around trouble along the way."

"She heard our conversation in the war room?" Dirk sat up, looking a little more alarmed.

"Like I said." I shrugged. "She's the third member of our crew. Where we go, she goes."

Elliot laughed again. "Cool."

"There is nothing cool about it," Dirk pressed. "Harboring an unknown entity in a restricted area is prohibited. I will have to notify General Pen the moment we return."

I nodded. "Fair enough. We weren't trying to keep anything secret."

"Go ahead and get us underway, Buttercup. Something tells me this is going to be a long trip."

EIGHT

"So, tell me how you become a Santa." I spun my chair to face Dirk on my left, trying to sound casual. Making small talk between Dirk and Elliot felt about as natural as mixing motor oil in your drinking water. We had been underway only a few hours, but it felt like an eternity. At least Buttercup had finished Elliot's chair. He now sat behind me, making our reverse triangle seating arrangement more of a diamond, though his position was somewhat elevated so he could see over me for a view of the forward screen.

"Do you have to go through special training, or do you just volunteer for the position?"

Bubbles was nestled sound asleep in my arm and Twitch had yet to show himself. He was probably camouflaged somewhere on the bridge and would glide in to make his entrance when the time was right.

"We are only known as Santa on Earth. On Deadala among the Dazbog we are known as ... Yule Rangers."

Dirk announced the title like a commercial for a Sunday night monster truck rally. My eyes bulged as I looked at Lois and tried not to burst out laughing. She had her hands over her face, scratching a conspicuous itch on her forehead.

Dirk didn't seem to notice our lack of reverence as he went on with his explanation.

"Yule Rangers must endure months of special forces training and complete a final assessment before being sent off-world on a deployment. Yule Rangers are given one chance to make it through the gauntlet. If he or she fails or quits before completing the course, they are deemed unfit to bear the name Yule Ranger forever."

It was so hard to take a big guy like Dirk seriously when he kept saying the words, Yule Ranger.

"One chance?" Lois had recovered from her erroneous itch and had her hands in her lap again. "That's pretty rough. What do you have to do?"

"The gauntlet is a series of overlapping trials in which you shoulder a pack of heavy gifts through dangerous obstacles. You must evade burning buildings, attack dogs, gunfire, attempts at capture, flash floods, hurricane and tornado force winds, natural gas asphyxiation, food poisoning, both intentional and accidental. The gauntlet was the most challenging experience I have ever faced in my entire life. I confess I barely made it out with my life."

I blinked. "You have to do all of that *and* carry a bag full of toys?"

"Weighing approximately one hundred fifty pounds, yes. Nothing is simulated. Every danger is real. Either you navigate the trials of the gauntlet and deliver the toys at the end or ... let's just say there are many Dazbog who are unsuccessful in the gauntlet."

"That's insane." Lois appeared every bit as shocked as I

was. "Why would you have to go through all of that to deliver toys to children?"

"It's one thing to deliver a toy to a child, it's quite another to break into a stranger's home in the middle of the night and creep around amongst sleeping families, even if they half expect you to be there. Humans, in particular, are unpredictable and violent when protecting their loved ones. While I commend your commitment to family, it makes the job of *Santa Claus* quite difficult and dangerous."

"Wow." I nodded. "I never considered how much went into getting that toy under the tree on Christmas."

I pondered the implications a moment longer, then my eyes went to Elliot sitting on his chair behind me. Buttercup had misjudged his height, so his feet dangled and didn't quite touch the floor. He had remained quiet throughout Dirk's story, something I had learned, he did not do very often.

"So how ... I mean are you going to have to ..." I appraised the spindly looking Dazbog wondering how he could ever make it through something that Dirk, the very embodiment of strength and fitness, had barely survived himself.

Elliot raised an eyebrow at me, seemingly content with watching me flounder. When I didn't come to any discernible conclusion, he held up a hand to stop my stammering.

"I may be an apprentice, but no Dazbog is allowed to embark on a deployment without completing the gauntlet and being granted the full title of Yule Ranger."

"So, you ..." Lois said. "But how ... I mean ..."

It seemed my stammering was contagious

"He cheated." Dirk spit out the words before Elliot had a chance to answer.

"I did not cheat." Elliot glared at Dirk. "Just because I'm

smarter than all the meathead puppets that zombie through and do everything the same way, doesn't mean I cheated."

"You hacked the entire system. How is that not cheating?"

Elliot ignored Dirk and turned his attention to Lois and me again. "Rather than lumber through it like an animal, I chose a more cerebral approach. I reprogrammed the twelve LF units responsible for facilitating the first obstacle and had them accompany me through the gauntlet. One carried my bag while the rest neutralized the threats. By the time I got to the end, I only had three units left but I walked out and made my delivery. And as you can see, I did not *hack* the entire system. I used the tools available to me and innovated a solution."

By the time he finished speaking I grinned so wide I could hardly contain my admiration for the little guy. Here he was, a third the size of Dirk, but I wouldn't bet against him in a fight. Dirk played by the book, and he did it well, but Elliot knew how to color outside the lines and there was a lot more space to play with when you were willing to use everything on the page.

"I think you both did an amazing job," Lois said. "I mean you came at it from different angles but—"

"Cheating is not an angle." Dirk interrupted, his eyes still on Elliot. "It's cheating. A Dazbog like him could never—"

"Could never what?" Elliot said, staring right back at him. "Could never complete the gauntlet? Well guess what, I did and I'm not afraid to do it again. How about you? You feel like going another round in the gauntlet, Dirk?"

Dirk stood and so did Elliot. I shot out of my chair and hurried between them with Bubbles still in my arm thinking I might have to toss her to Lois just to keep her out of harm's way.

A familiar pressure on my shoulder stopped me. Twitch

materialized into a bright red ball of fury and hissed at Dirk who in turn reared away in surprise.

"What is that?" Dirk said, forgetting his argument with Elliot for the moment.

Twitch scurried over and hissed at Elliot as well, but he reacted with less surprise.

"Is that a Chitterwall?" Elliot's face went from anger, to bewilderment, to wonder in the span of a couple of seconds. "Where did you find him?"

"He's the unofficial guardian on this bridge," I said. "And if there is any fighting, you will have to deal with him."

Elliot let out a little chuckle and extended a tentative hand in his direction. Twitch hissed and lunged at him, clacking his little teeth in a mock attempt to bite his fingers.

"Okay, no need to get testy."

"We have a long trip ahead of us and a mission with lots of kids' lives on the line." I looked at Elliot then Dirk. "You two need to put away your differences and figure out how to work as a team, at least on this mission. I won't have this whole thing fall apart just because you two don't like each other. Get it together. You're supposed to be Yule Rangers. Act like it."

I couldn't believe I had used the words Yule Rangers in a serious sentence, but it seemed to work. They both nodded and sat in their seats, not quite apologizing, but at least they weren't trying to kill each other either.

"Good. Now let's try to—"

"I hate to interrupt this little group therapy session," Buttercup said, cutting me off. "But we may have a small problem. I am sensing a ship on an intercept course, and they appear to have their shields and weapons systems active. I believe it is a Cur ship and they are moving in for an attack."

NINE

I spun to look at the forward screen and saw a strange crescent-shaped ship heading our direction. It had curved forward facing wings like a crescent moon, and the fuselage jutted out of the center making it resemble a stylized letter E. I could not imagine the functional advantage of such a design, but the sandy beige hull and orange lighting gave it an ancient Egyptian feel, even though we were about as far from the Nile as we could get.

"Missile lock," Buttercup announced. "Engaging shields. Taking evasive action."

Everyone dove for their seats as stars spun across the screen. Even Twitch had taken his place at the top of my chair. Inertia dampeners transferred very little of the movement to the inside of the ship, but during maneuvers this extreme we still felt the force of her turns.

Automatic restraints rolled out of the seats to buckle us in and I saw the virtual weapons control display appear in front of Lois out of the corner of my eye.

"Switch to Battlesight," I ordered. "I want to see who we're dealing with."

Without warning, the entire deck melted away into a near three-sixty view of the space around us. In less than a second, it was like our chairs were floating unhindered through the firefight with nothing but the virtual displays and data screens to orient us.

"Wow." Elliot shouted from behind me. "How did you manage that?"

"I don't care about how." Dirk had his feet off the floor, holding them in the air, presumably because he believed the floor was no longer there. "Next time warn us before you do something like that."

"Sorry," I said. "No time for explanations. Buttercup, are you a match for that ship's battlements?"

Buttercup let out a chilling laugh I had never heard before. I wasn't sure how I felt about it.

"Against a Scavid battle cruiser we may be outmatched, but I was made for a fight like this. That Cur fighter doesn't stand a chance."

As she said it, Buttercup spun again, twisting the missiles on our tail into a collision that ended in a brilliant explosion.

"Now it's my turn." Buttercup changed her trajectory so fast I felt it in my seat. One second the Cur ship was gaining ground behind us, the next we were looping around into attack position on her port side.

"Energy cannon and rail gun." I pointed at Lois who had her hands hovering over the weapons control display.

The Cur ship tried to peel off to starboard, but Buttercup was far faster and more maneuverable.

Bright green bolts of energy pounded into the side of the Cur ship and our rail gun tore a hole in the crescent section of the ship. I spun my chair to look behind us as we passed the crippled ship. Orange lights blinked in erratic patterns then went out all over the port side crescent and main hull.

"You can't let them go," Dirk said. "If you allow them to survive, they'll self-repair and contact their fleet. You might be a match for this ship, but I doubt you could outfly a dozen of them."

"Try me," Buttercup challenged, and brought us around to an attack position again.

The Cur ship was wounded and flying on a straight course, but it wasn't helpless. If we were stupid enough to swing around in range of her guns, she could still bite.

"Can we disable the ship?" I turned toward Lois.

"Sure we can, but is that the best thing for us to do?" She seemed as unsure as I was.

Fighting an armed, capable enemy was one thing. Firing on a helpless ship with a full crew was another.

"I can't believe I'm saying this, but Dirk is right," Elliot said from behind me. "If you allow them to go free, they'll intercept us with enough reinforcements to finish the job."

I turned from Lois to peer forward again. "Buttercup, can you jam their communications?"

"Already done," Buttercup said. "Though they may have called for reinforcements before they engaged, and my jamming capabilities will cease the moment we leave the area."

I groaned, staring at the hapless ship not knowing what to do. Buttercup had brought us into a position behind them ready to fire the moment I gave the command. My mind raced for a solution, then an idea hit me.

"Do you think they have a Void Prism onboard?"

"It's likely they do." Elliot answered before Dirk could. "The Cur don't have a dominating space fleet by galactic standards, but what they do have are the Void Prisms. They're the only ones who know where to mine them, and if they can get close enough to a planet to invade, a single Cur becomes millions in the span of a second. A few hundred Cur could overwhelm any ground force known throughout the universe. In a time of war, it would make sense for every ship to carry at least one so they could deploy ground troops if necessary."

I shifted my gaze to Dirk and gave him a hard look. "If we can disable that ship, how do you feel about forming a boarding party to get that Prism?"

Dirk's features turned dark and very un-Santa like. "The Cur rely on numbers. They're poor hand to hand fighters. They would not be able to use the prism to their advantage either. The space would be far too small to accommodate that many Cur without destroying their ship. I believe we can take them without much of a problem."

"Wait," Lois said. "What are we talking about here?"

I spun to face her.

"We take out their ship with an EMP warhead, board and steal a Void Prism. We'll have what we need to complete our mission, and the Cur won't be able to contact any other ships in time to intercept us. It's a win. win."

"Except for the hand-to-hand fighting part." She peered over her glasses. "Did you miss that?"

"Come on. There are kids' lives at stake. Not just a few. All of them. We have to try."

Lois groaned and glanced at Bubbles. I still had her cradled in my arm. Through all the yelling and excitement, she hadn't woken up. What if she was going through a growth spurt or something? I didn't even want to know what that might look like.

"Okay." She let out an exasperated breath. "It seems like

we have no choice." Her voice got a little louder, "but don't forget about the kid we have right here. We need to take care of her too."

I nodded and smiled. "How could I forget? She's what got us here in the first place."

"Well then, Captain," Lois said, "Let's do this."

I spun my chair to face forward again and eyed the Cur ship limping helpless through space.

"Buttercup, bring us around and arm an EMP warhead. Lois, target their bridge. We want to be sure to knock out all their communications. We only have one shot at this. Let's be smart and get out with the goods. If we're lucky, they won't even know we were there."

TEN

E veryone stood in a circle on the bridge making final preparations to board the Cur Ship. Twitch rode on my shoulder, ready for anything, and Bubbles was cradled in Lois' arms giggling at the lot of us. Buttercup had disengaged Battle-sight mode so her cavernous-looking hull was now visible again. I had my revolver set to stun, but I was ready to dial it up and deliver more of a lethal punch if I had to. I couldn't stop thinking about all the kids on Earth and how their lives would be snuffed out if we failed in our mission. I wasn't the type of person who went in guns blazing, but this was a case where failure was not an option. We needed to get that Void Prism no matter the risk ... or the cost.

"I'm not trying to insult you" I appraised Dirk and his apparent lack of offensive tools, "but I'm sure the Cur will have some sort of weaponry. Shouldn't you carry something to defend yourself."

"The Yule Rangers do not deploy unarmed." Dirk raised his arm to touch the inner portion of three gold rings he wore on his forearm and a curved shield of blue/white light came to life in front of him. It spanned almost head to toe and reminded me of a roman style scutum. Dirk's mountainous form crouched behind that shield would make anyone think twice before attacking, and he would be a formattable battering ram the moment he decided to charge forward.

"Okay then. Dirk and I will go in. Lois and Elliot, you stay back as a retrieval team in case things go south."

I turned to look at Twitch on my shoulder. "You can come with us. If we're going in to steal something, it can't hurt to have the galaxy's best thief on our side."

Twitch chittered and let out a little growl of determination that made me laugh.

"I still believe this is a fool's errand," Elliot protested. "There are far better ways to infiltrate an enemy compound than charging through the front door."

"I appreciate your opinion, but we've been over this," I said, feeling a little of Dirk's frustration at Elliot's lack of fortitude. "We can't override the ships systems because they have no power to override. All their computers are down, and even if they weren't, I'm not so sure I like your idea to flood the ship with gas before we go in. What if we don't vent it properly afterwards or what if the gas is flammable? We might blow the ship to smithereens before we find the prism."

"Ridiculous." Elliot pouted. "A carbon monoxide saturation would never explode, and you could wear respirators if you feared exposure. I'm sure Buttercup has the ability to monitor atmospheric conditions."

I sighed. "It still doesn't change the fact that we have no way to flood the ship without control over the life support systems. They'll barely survive as it is without us pumping all their air into space."

"If you had conferred with me before firing your EMP, I could have taken control of—"

"Okay," I said, interrupting him a little louder than I meant to. "I get it. I'm sorry your plan won't work this time, but this is what we're going with."

Lois cocked an eyebrow at me and grinned.

"What?" I said. "You got the hard job. You have to keep Bubbles distracted enough to stop her from folding to me. It's going to be way too dangerous for her in there."

"I'll do my best." She shrugged and rocked the little Viraquin in her arms. "But you may want to bring your backpack just in case. If she decides to fold, there isn't much I can do about it."

I sighed. "You're probably right. Hey, before we go, can you tell me what this Void Prism looks like? If we need to split up, I'd like to know what I'm looking for. Where would they keep something like that?"

"The Void Prism is extremely dangerous," Elliot said. "If it were to fracture or become unstable, the results can be catastrophic. They would keep it in a safe place. Likely in a designated case or maybe even a vault. Probably on the bridge or in the captain's quarters."

"Okay, at least we have a place to start searching. What does it look like?"

Buttercup materialized an image on the forward screen, and I almost laughed out loud when I laid eyes on it. "You have got to be kidding me."

There, floating on the screen, was an image of an honest to goodness snow globe. It didn't have a depiction of the North Pole or the Statue of Liberty inside, but rather a crystal-clear wedge of glass with a faint purple hue and snowflakes swirled all around it in a thick white flurry that never settled to the bottom.

"This is how the prism will appear in its dormant form," Buttercup explained. "The moving aggregate inside the globe prevents the prism from focusing onto a target and splitting mass similar to the way a regular prism splits light. To activate the Void Prism, the globe is shattered, releasing the aggregate and freeing the prism to split the subject within its range. The prism will last twenty-four hours before degrading, and then it is useless."

I let the description sink in as I stared at the image.

"Yeah, but it's a snow globe."

I looked at Lois and her face was a mix of amusement and disbelief as well. "I haven't seen one of those since I was a kid," she said.

"Me either." I thought back, trying to remember a time a place when I had seen one last. "I think my mom got me one for Christmas. It had the Batmobile with Batman and Robin. Too bad it's not that easy to get one with a Void Prism."

I laughed at the strange irony as I stared at the screen.

"Don't you even think about it, young lady." Lois' voice cut through my reminiscing.

When I turned my head, I could already see the tell-tale signs of Bubbles' power beginning to go to work. The bioluminescence in her skin began to grow bright, then she turned white as everything started to bend around her. Space seemed to bow and stretch, and I had just enough time to say "Oh sh ..." Then we were gone.

ELEVEN

A cacophony of hiccups erupted on the bridge as we popped out of the fold to an unknown location in the vast expanse of space.

"Bubbles." I glared down at the giggling little Viraquin in Lois' arms. "What ... hic ... did you do?"

"I smell bread. How can someone be baking?" Dirk was half crouched to the ground as if he couldn't decide whether to run or fight. "Somebody tell me ... hic ... what just happened."

"Smells and hiccups are a si ... hic ... side effect of *folding through space.*" Lois annunciated that last part, looking at Bubbles to scold her with the words. "I smell fresh ... hic ... cut flowers."

"Fold?" Elliot straightened and looked toward the front viewscreen. "Fold ... hic ... where?"

I looked at the screen as well, doing my best to breathe through my mouth. At the moment, the only thing I smelled was an eye watering skunk.

"And I smell ... hic ... peppermint," Elliot amended. "Not bread or flowers."

"Of course, you do." I rolled my eyes.

Somehow, I always got the stink while everyone else got baked goods and roses.

Dirk rose from his ready position, but he was still wound tight as a cat. "How long ... hic... does this last?"

"Not long," Lois offered him a strained smile. "They will go away in a sec ... hic ... second."

"Hey." I squinted at a shadowy object tumbling in space outside the ship. "I think we may have a bigger problem to wor ... hic ... worry about than hiccups." I couldn't quite make it out, but something was approaching fast and it didn't look friendly. An alert sounded on the bridge, then a collision from somewhere behind us forced me to grab the back of my chair to steady myself.

"Buttercup, what was that?" I shouted. "Are you okay?"

The perspective on the screen shifted as she took evasive action and more of the objects came into view, crossing and converging across our path.

"Not precisely." Buttercup's voice sounded strained, as if she were concentrating too hard to answer.

"It seems ..."

Another impact. This one sent us spinning around off axis in a violent jolt.

"You may want to sit down," Buttercup blurted out. "It seems we have folded into the middle of an asteroid field. Escape might not be poss ..."

A third blow, this one not quite as hard as the last, had us diving for our seats. Twitch still crouched on my shoulder and Lois had Bubbles in her arms. The moment I sat down, Twitch took his place above me and Lois held on to the little Viraquin, keeping her safe as well.

"Don't bother finishing that last statement," I said. "Just do your best to get us out of here."

The image on the forward screen twisted and shifted as if we had a first-person view through the eyes of a hummingbird. I considered having her switch to Battlesight, but I had a feeling we were better off not seeing what was out there trying to kill us.

Buttercup barrel-rolled and dove under an asteroid, but another appeared out of nowhere behind it and she barely avoided hitting it head on. It still impacted our starboard side hard enough to overcome the inertia dampeners and we all had to brace ourselves to avoid being thrown out of our seats.

"Shields are at twenty percent." Buttercup announced over the speakers, sounding desperate and almost breathless even though she was a computer. "We have lost the starboard engine and the Warpstream drive is down. I have a hull breach in the aft section, but I have isolated and sealed the area."

Another barrel-roll to avoid an asteroid that threatened to shear off the top of our ship.

"We have to get out of here." I said, stating the obvious. "Do we still have weapons? Can we target some of the asteroids and blast them out of the way?"

Virtual weapon's control displays appeared in front of all four chairs, and I did not waste any time targeting anything in our path. Lois and Elliot did the same and while it took Dirk took a little longer to orient himself, he was blasting away within a few moments as well. Each of us had control of either an energy cannon or rail gun, and for a second I feared we created more debris than we cleared. Then I saw where Buttercup was headed, and everyone redoubled their efforts to cut her a path.

Buttercup looped around and rocketed for the outer edge,

but an asteroid more than a mile wide surged in front of us. It seemed impossible anything that big could move so fast. The four of us concentrated our fire without speaking, drilling into the center of the asteroid. Two skipper missiles streaked out of the hull in front of us and impacted the surface, detonating seismic charges at the target location as well. When they did, the colossal rock finally ruptured.

Buttercup never even slowed. Instead, she turned us on a vertical axis and split the gap like a knife through butter. The moment we were free everyone let out a cheer loud enough to be heard back on Earth.

"We did it!" Lois jumped out of her chair in excitement, and I followed suit.

"That was fast thinking with the skipper missiles." I grinned. "You are getting to be quite the weapons officer."

"Thanks." She nodded at me. "I should have asked for permission to fire but there was no time."

"You saved all our lives." I turned to see Elliot and Dirk were on their feet too. "That and Buttercup's amazing dogfighting skills."

"Dogfighting implies we were in direct conflict with a hostile force." Buttercup was back to her impassive self. "Evasive maneuvers would be more accurate, though if anyone else were piloting, the probability that you would have been mashed to human paste would be almost one hundred percent."

I glanced at Dirk and Elliot. "Sorry, Buttercup is usually a little more inclusive. I'm sure she meant you would be Dazbog paste, too."

Lois still had Bubbles in her arm, but the baby didn't look quite so giggly and gleeful anymore. I had a feeling she had sensed the tension and urgency in the air, even if she didn't know she was the cause of it.

"You, young lady, are in big trouble." I pointed at Bubbles and then realized once again, that I had no idea how to discipline a baby Viraquin. When I didn't say anything else, Lois rolled her eyes and set Bubbles on her chair, turning her away from the rest of the group.

"Time out for you," she said in a stern voice. "Stay there until we say you can come ou—"

Before she finished the sentence there was a flash of bright light and Bubbles appeared out of thin air, right in front of my face. I reached out and caught her before she could fall and Bubbles giggled and cooed, making her bioluminescent waves dance and flow over her skin.

"That's great," I said. "Now what?"

"Put her down again until she stops folding."

"And what if she decides to fold away altogether or folds us somewhere even more dangerous because she's mad. This is not a toddler in preschool. She's a baby Viraquin. She doesn't even understand what using her power did to us a few seconds ago."

"There still has to be consequences, or she will never learn." Lois growled the statement in her gravely serious voice.

"Okay, but we have to find a way that won't cause more trouble."

"Sometimes," Lois glared at me. "You have to make a little trouble to teach a child not to create it."

"Excuse me." We both jerked our heads toward Elliot and saw that he and Dirk were staring at us.

"I don't mean to interrupt." Elliot's voice was cool and calm, with an edge of sarcasm. "But can we focus on something a little larger than time-out for the baby? How about we start with something small like, *where we are* or *what's the damage to the ship?*"

I blinked then shook my head. "You're right. This isn't important right now."

I looked at Lois. She nodded, although her expression told me we would return to this problem later.

"Buttercup, can you get a fix on our location?"

"Negative."

I paused as we all stared at each other. Bio-intelligence, AI or computer intelligence, it didn't matter. Negative should not be the answer when you ask a navigational system to track your location.

"What do you mean by negative?"

"I mean the location in which we now find ourselves is not on any of my navigational charts. It will take me some time to work out where we are according to astrological indicators."

"How is this possible?" Dirk's voice seemed on the edge of panic. "We have to go back. I have to complete my mission. How are we ever going to get to Earth in time?"

That was enough to trip my panic button as well. We had been so busy dodging our own deaths I had momentarily forgotten about the kids on Earth. How would we get back in time to save them? Dirk was right. We were in far more trouble now than before.

"Can we send General Pen a message?" Lois said, picking up on the sudden urgency as well. "Maybe he can dispatch another Santa ... er Yule Ranger."

"Not possible," Buttercup said. "I am not sure of our precise location, but being at the edge of uncharted space also means we are out of communications range. Even if we could transmit a message, it would only be a homing beacon for the Cur and a signal to track us or anyone else they might send in our place."

"It doesn't matter. No other Ranger would take the mission

anyway." Elliot's eyes were cast to the ground in defeat, but Dirk turned a glare in his direction.

"Speak for yourself. I was proud to be chosen for such a distinguished—"

"You were chosen because no one else wanted it."

Lois and I stared at Elliot, barely able to believe the words that had come out of his mouth.

"Please don't take any offense." He glanced up to meet our horrified expressions. "I like you two. I like humans, but Earth is a violent and inhospitable place for us. All the shootings and traps and biting."

"Biting?" I said.

"Yeah. Dogs. They are the bane of every Yule Ranger's deployment. I swear every house has a dog that wants to chew your face off. It doesn't even matter if we bring them treats. Your mailman has nothing on Santa when it comes to dogs. Dirk would have graduated at the top of his class, but he has impulse control issues. They almost kicked him out of the academy, except he agreed to take Earth as his primary deployment."

Dirk lunged for Elliot, hands outstretched for his throat. To Elliot's credit he didn't cringe or cower away. He just turned to face him, even though Dirk was three times his size.

Thankfully the only person needed to thwart the attack was Dirk. He seemed to regain his senses and stop before he throttled his loquacious companion, lowering his hands to his side through a noticeable effort of will.

"All that is behind me now." Dirk's face was beet red, and he spoke through gritted teeth, but his voice was calm and even. "I have overcome that darker side of myself and I now strive to prove my worth through service to the Rangers."

Seeing Dirk like this made me glad I didn't know him *before* he had control over his anger.

"Well, I for one am honored that both of you are willing and able to go to Earth and help all of those children." Lois stepped forward, and much to my surprise, hugged the red-faced Dirk, then did the same for Elliot. "Despite all the dogs and the more enthusiastic home defenders, I would like to thank you, and I hope when this is all over, you're both recognized for your hard work."

I wasn't much of a hugger, but I stepped forward and offered my hand instead. "I'm not quite as eloquent as Lois, but the same goes for me." I shook their hands and by the time Lois and I stepped back, they had both lost their combative air.

"You're welcome." Dirk dipped his head in a self-conscious gesture and Elliot did the same. "I only wish we could be there to do more right now."

I sighed and nodded my head with frustration, then turned toward the forward screen. I still had Bubbles in my arm, so I sat her in my chair. Twitch scurried over to sit with her, no doubt to keep her busy and prevent another erroneous folding.

"Any luck on our location yet, Buttercup? And while you're at it, how about a status report on the damage we sustained in the asteroid field."

"Our shields are down at the moment, as is our starboard engine and the Warpstream drive. We sustained major hull damage to the exterior of the ship, but by some miracle the only breach was in the aft section. The good news is our power generator and life support are fully operational. Given time and available power distribution, my onboard fabricators should be able to break down and remanufacture all the damaged components to facilitate a full repair."

"Well, that's some good news," I said. "What about our location?"

"I believe I have pinpointed our location in an uncharted section of the Caroga system. It is far past the outreach of any established settlements and would take us months, perhaps years to return using the Warpstream drive."

"Years?" Lois walked up next to me. "We don't have years."

Her eyes went to Bubbles, and I shook my head. I knew what she was thinking. Bubbles was our only hope to get home, but her folds were random and inconsistent at best. There seemed to be no real rhyme or reason to her actions.

"Do we have any other options?" I said, hoping for any other Hail Mary.

"I am not sure this is an option to return home any sooner, but I have made an interesting discovery."

The viewscreen switched to the surface of an inhospitable looking planet. The ground was black and rocky, devoid of almost all life. The only distinguishing characteristics were the huge volcanic fissures that ran across the entire surface like veins in a living organism. The color was strange too. The rivers of molten rock were not bright orange in the way you might expect, but rather glowing purple and blue. It was beautiful in a raw and violent way. Not a place I'd want to spend a summer vacation, but a fascinating place to see on the screen.

"This is the planet we are currently orbiting. Considering the inhospitable nature on the surface, I did not expect to find any signs of life, but I was surprised to find a rather unusual amount of automated orbital and ground security. In fact, if we had entered orbit in any other place we may have been blown out of the sky before we knew what happened."

"Why would a place like this have security?" Elliot said. "Could someone be living down there? Maybe subsurface?"

"You are closer than you might think," Buttercup answered. "I have detected some unusual mining activity on the far side of the planet. I managed a low-level scan without alerting their security."

"So, what are they mining?" I was tired of all this cat and mouse. Buttercup was stalling and that could mean only one thing. This was big ... and it would likely drop us into some hot water.

"This is somewhat of a good news bad news situation."

"Fine." I sighed. "Good news first."

"The good news is we have found the long-hidden Void Prism mine of the Cur."

Dirk jetted forward to look at the screen as though he would be able to see the mine hidden on the surface.

"We have to get down there. If that is the Void Prism mine, it is our responsibility to take it, or at least collect as many prisms as we can and then return with reinforcements."

"Therein lies the bad news," Buttercup said. "Going to that mine would be ..." She paused for a moment as if searching for the right word. "Inadvisable."

"What do you mean inadvisable?" I asked.

"In addition to a myriad of automated defense systems, the mine is protected by the most vicious species known in this universe. That mine is guarded by the dreaded Unicorns."

TWELVE

"We must attempt to retrieve the Void Prisms." Dirk said it more like an announcement than a request or simple statement.

I stared at the flowing veins of purple-blue lava on the screen. "What is the atmosphere like on the surface?"

"You are not actually considering this," Lois said. "I'm all for helping, and I will do about anything to save all those kids, but this sounds like suicide. We can't even get back to Earth in time to do any good."

"We have a possibility, and you know it." My eyes drifted to Bubbles. "If we can decode this little bundle of giggling madness, we can make it in plenty of time. All we need is a prism."

Lois' lips tightened into a thin line, but she knew I was right. The chance might be slim, but with the lives of every child on Earth at stake, a slim chance, even one full of danger, beat no chance at all.

"I'm afraid I'm with Lois this time."

I turned to gawk at the screen where Buttercup's vocal sine wave overlaid the video feed.

"Are you serious? You're always the one eager to pillage and plunder. Attack and explode. Those are your specialties."

"Not when Unicorns are involved. They are bloodthirsty savages. They do not care about anything but carnage. They prefer handheld weapons because they like to see their victims die. They are known for inflicting torture so unspeakable even the Scavid avoid them."

"We can steer clear of any confrontation," Dirk said. "Instead of taking the mine, we'll only procure the Void Prisms we need for now. We have the location. We can always come back later. I believe we can infiltrate with a simple plan and escape without detection."

I stared at him for a moment considering.

"This is all rash and impulsive," Elliot said. "We should think this through. I can figure out a way to hack their automated defense systems, then maybe we can find a way to turn their weapons against them."

I shook my head. "That will take too long and all they'll do is retreat into the mine for cover, which is the very place we want to be."

"Perhaps Buttercup can fabricate some sort of drilling apparatus. We can—"

"Is your plan simple?" I looked at Dirk as I cut Elliot off and he nodded once.

"We can get in and out. All we need is a distraction."

"What sort of distraction?" Buttercup sounded interested for the first time. She may not think going against the Unicorns was a good idea, but the allure of a good old fashioned pirate raid proved too much for her to resist.

Dirk grinned. "The exploding kind would be best."

There was a pause, then. "It will take some time to facilitate my repairs anyway. ART can assist me during your absence, so I see no problem acting as a subtle distraction for your plan."

"I think we're going for something a little less than subtle," I said.

"I meant subtle for me," Buttercup said. "For you it will seem more like a small-scale war."

"Who is Art?" Lois tilted her head and I realized she had never seen the automated maintenance drone Buttercup had onboard. As if on cue, the Golden Retriever sized ant clacked into the room on its metal legs and stood at the bulkhead door.

Lois screamed ... Dirk screamed. Elliot crouched to the ground and held out his hand out as if he were calling the family dog.

"This is ART," Buttercup announced. "My Autonomous Repair Technician. He will facilitate any repairs I cannot do myself."

"Has that thing been on the ship the whole time?" Lois looked like she might jump up and stand on her chair.

"Of course," Buttercup said. "He is docked in a module in the cargo hold and can be deployed when necessary."

"Okay, well just keep him away from me."

"ART is harmless." I detected a hint of mischievousness in Buttercup's voice and the giant metal ant took a step forward.

"I'm serious!" Lois' voice got low and gravely the way it did just before things got ugly.

Dirk managed to fall back several steps, putting more distance between him and the mechanical insect.

"As you wish."

ART turned around and headed back the way he had

come, and Lois relaxed. I raised an eyebrow at Dirk and he cleared his throat, taking a few steps forward again.

"Bugs," he said. "They're a thing for me."

I nodded and tried not to grin too wide, then my eyes went to Lois. "Can we get back to the matter at hand? I think grabbing a Prism is the right call. We can even bring Twitch. He's great at stealing things. You know he's in."

Twitch skittered up from the seat next to Bubbles to stand on the back of the chair and chitter his concurrence.

Lois turned to Elliot. "What do you think? You're the analytical one in the group. What's our best chance?"

Elliot lost his grin and looked at each of us in turn, seeming more than a little surprised that anyone asked his opinion. Dirk even held his tongue to hear what the little Dazbog had to say.

Elliot sighed. "Much as I hate to admit it, Dirk and Ben both make good points. We might have a chance to sneak in and out if there is a distraction effective enough to draw the guards out of the area. Considering they believe the location is still a secret, they will not be expecting an attack. It's likely the Unicorns are there to keep the miners in check, not guard the mine from intruders."

"That's it, then. Dirk, make your plan and tell Buttercup what you need her to do. The four of us will go in and—"

Dirk held up a hand. "Hold on. I'm going in alone. You three stay on the ship. I will go in, steal the prisms and then you can pick me up."

I laughed until I realized he was serious. "Not a chance. I'm going in with you. What if something goes wrong? There's no way you're going in there alone."

"And I'm not staying behind either." Lois grinned. "There's no way the boys get to hog all the glory."

All eyes went to Elliot. The deafening silence grew until he groaned in defeat. "Fine. But I'm not going in empty-handed. I'm bringing some of my gear with me. You never know where we might need it."

I nodded. "Excellent. As soon as we're ready with a plan, we'll head to the planet for the raid."

I smiled with confidence, but inside I quaked in my boots. I knew this was a crazy idea. If these Unicorns were as bad as Buttercup said, I doubted we would be a match for one, much less a whole gang. All we could do is hope Buttercup's distraction would be good enough to get in and back out alive.

THIRTEEN

My first experience setting foot on an alien planet was not a pleasant one. Technically it was my second experience, but the Dazbog planet was so covered in mechanized machinery, it felt more like a space station. This place, however, remained raw, wild and untouched by advanced alien technology.

The sandy, black soil seemed to absorb the light, and true to the aerial images of the landscape, we found little to no vegetation. The one sad plant that did take root was a strange red vine with lots of tiny leaves. It crawled along the blackened ground in long snaking lengths and Buttercup warned us not to touch it lest our skin would burn like fire for days without relief.

It was possible to breathe the air, but the odor of ammonia overwhelmed our olfactory senses all the way to our eyeballs and the sweltering heat only made it worse. Buttercup provided us respirators in case we found the smell intolerable. One eye-watering whiff had us all fumbling like a bunch of teargassed protesters to breathe through anything that would cut the horrible aroma.

The smell and the heat weren't the only bad things, either. A whipping wind blew sand into our eyes, ears and pretty much any area exposed to the elements. Since sweat poured out of every inch of my body, the dry black sand stuck to my skin like glitter on a kindergartener's art project. The strange bluish-purple lava flows seemed responsible for most of the delightful environment. Not only was it the source of the sand and heat, but also the bionic cat urine that would give me nightmares for the next three weeks.

"How long is it going to take for your ship to produce that distraction?" Dirk's voice sounded muted by the respirator, and though I stood right next to him, it was difficult to hear him over the howling wind.

He and Elliot knelt next to me behind one of the many sandstone formations that riddled the landscape. The place sort of reminded me of Moab, Utah, only hot, sandy and uninviting ... okay, it was exactly like Moab, Utah.

"I don't know." I tried to balance my voice between a shout and remaining quiet enough to stay hidden. "I can't even tell if anyone's inside the mine."

I glanced at Lois who crouched on the other side of Elliot. She raised a finger, then dug into the magic purse draped across her body. In less than a second she pulled out a tiny clamshell case, and when she popped it open, it became a miniature pair of binoculars.

I blinked at her as she tried to hand them to me.

"What?" She said, "They're vintage."

I took the miniature optics and peered into the mouth of the cave in front of us. Much to my surprise, they did offer an improved view. I swear, that purse has everything.

"The coast looks clear right now, but Buttercup told us to

wait. She said we wouldn't miss ... whatever it is she plans to do."

Twitch huddled on my shoulder shielding his face from the sand. Buttercup said the acrid atmosphere wouldn't bother him or Bubbles who rode in her armored carrier on my back. Still, I couldn't help but wonder if she was all right.

"You can tell your compatriot that I am almost ready," Buttercup broke in, speaking over our internal communication system. Lois and I were the only ones who could hear. Dirk and Elliot could not. "My cloaking device seems to be hiding me from the automated defense systems, but the moment I provide your distraction I will be exposed. I must be sure I am in a position to defend myself."

"Okay." I glanced at Lois, and she nodded. "Just be careful."

Dirk never took his eyes off the mine in front of us. "Well? What did she say?"

"She's almost ready." I handed the binoculars back to Lois and she tucked them into her purse. "It should only be a few minutes."

Dirk answered with a single nod and I turned to peer over our outcropping. The mine was nothing special to see from the exterior. The black sand made it difficult to see the similar colored tailings left outside the opening, and the only piece of heavy machinery I saw was a squat sort of tug with a single cart attached to the rear. To the casual observer, the site could belong to a survey crew or a research team. But we knew better. Buttercup had confirmed the existence of a vast tunnel network and multiple life forms inside. That, and the confirmation of the ultra-rare element that produced the Void Prism, made the location of the mine unmistakable.

As we waited, a figure emerged from the tunnel. We all

crouched a little lower to remain out of sight, but I squinted at the newcomer regretting that I had returned Lois' binoculars. The alien appeared grotesque, with features that resembled a bat. It had four eyes, large ears, long spindly arms, and it crept along the ground as if it were sneaking up on some sort of prey. It wore rags for clothing that barely covered its leathery looking skin, and I could see a tuft of brown fur that poked out of a worn red and blue shell it wore as a helmet.

"Is that a Unicorn?" I couldn't believe this haggard looking creature could be the fierce predator Buttercup had described. Maybe years in the mine had changed it somehow.

"No." Elliot peeked over the sandstone. "*That* is a Unicorn."

He nodded toward the opening of the mine and my eyes widened at the gigantic hulking figure stomping out of the darkness. This creature had an unmistakable equestrian head with a long, spiraled horn, but that was where the comparisons to Earth lore ended. His neck was long and muscular, and he walked upright with a torso more gorilla than human. Wiry black hair covered most of his body, leading all the way down to the two powerful equine legs and hooved feet. He had a mane that stood out from his head and neck like a long manicured mohawk, and in his hands was a weapon I'd never seen before. It resembled a huge, medieval, four-bladed mace with an inlaid musket-style pistol grip and trigger. I could only assume when he wasn't bashing someone's brains in, he could fire an energy bolt and kill his victim at range. In my hands it would have looked like a boat oar, but he held it in one fist as if it were a toy.

The hulking Unicorn walked over to the Bat Slave and snatched the cowering creature by its neck. Without a word, he threw it toward the mine, sending the Bat Slave sailing several feet in a rolling tumble before it regained its feet to run back into the tunnel. The Unicorn snorted out of his huge nostrils and watched the Bat Slave retreat. There was no shouting, no begging, no reprimand. Just the physical altercation and reaction. It was both the most terrifying and infuriating thing anyone could ever see. These slaves were little more than dogs to the Unicorns that kept them. Not worth the words it took to scold them.

The Unicorns were also every bit the hulking barbarian Buttercup said they would be, and more ... much more. More than my limited human brain could have imagined until now.

"Maybe we should rethink this plan," I whispered. "We don't even know how many of those things are in th—"

Before I could finish the sentence, an explosion rocked the blackened desert. A huge smoke cloud rose into the air among a rocky outcropping of hills and the reaction from the Unicorns was almost instant.

"I located a secondary entrance to the mine." Buttercup sounded calm and collected considering she had just called the entire planet's defenses down on her head. "I sent several shots into the main tunnel and collapsed the interior. I also had ART lay a seismic warhead outside. I will detonate it remotely when the Unicorns arrive, but I doubt it will neutralize them all. I will not be able to fire on them without revealing my position, and the automated defense systems are now on full alert. The moment my cloaking system is deactivated, they will fire on me, and their defense systems are formidable."

"Okay." I looked at Lois, still feeling unsure about the mission.

Her eyes grew big and she shrunk lower to the ground. "Here they come."

The four of us sat and watched a whole fleet of Unicorns

charge out of the mine. At least a dozen warriors, all armed with those brain-bashing space rifles.

I cringed. "Maybe we should hold back to be sure there are no other—"

Before I could finish. Dirk took off running toward the mine.

"Or we could go running in and hope we don't die."

Twitch latched onto my shoulder, and I launched out of our hiding space behind him. Lois and Elliot followed, and together we charged into the mine hoping we wouldn't run into a Unicorn surprise party waiting for us inside.

FOURTEEN

The moment we were inside the mine I knew we had made a mistake. Shafts ran off in every direction and more shafts branched off those. It was a labyrinth of carved black sandstone and we had no way of knowing which way to go. The walls were shored with some type of plastic sheeting that glowed yellow and lit the mine. There were no heavy structural supports, just endless row after row of the lit plastic arches, lighting our way into hopeless obscurity.

The good news was, we didn't see any Unicorns, at least not for the moment. Sooner or later, they would figure out Buttercup's distraction had been a ruse, and they would come running to defend the main entrance to the mine. If we weren't gone by then, things would get ugly for us real fast.

"Should we split up?" Dirk suggested. "Cover more ground and meet back here?"

"No way." I shook my head. "We have no idea what we're going to run into and there are too many shafts to cover them all anyway."

"What, then?" Lois threw out her hands in frustration. "We can't just stand here."

"If I may." Elliot held up a finger. "I might suggest we follow this shaft."

He turned and pointed to the shaft in front of us. "It's not only the largest one, indicating it likely leads to some sort of central hub, but I can also hear activity coming from that direction. If we want to find a Void Prism, it will be where they're working, not in a section they have closed."

We all stopped to listen, turning our heads toward the larger shaft. Sure enough, Elliot was right. The noise was faint, but I could hear the tell-tale sounds of heavy machinery echoing off the walls.

"It's better than nothing." I looked at everyone for agreement and they all nodded. Even Twitch chittered his concurrence.

"Okay let's go."

The four of us hurried down the shaft single file, hugging the right-side wall. There was no place to hide, no rocks or machinery to dive behind if someone came around the corner. The wall lent us nothing more than a false sense of security, but a false sense felt better than no sense at all.

I led the crew, followed by Lois, then Dirk and Elliot brought up the rear. Twitch sat on my shoulder and Bubbles rode in my pack. The gang was all here. Sand masked the sound of our footsteps, so it was easy for us to move quickly, but it wasn't long before our false sense of security shattered as one of the Bat Slaves crept around a corner ahead of us.

The four of us froze, watching the Bat Slave approach from the other side of the shaft. Now that I was closer to it, I could see that the thing was smaller than I thought. Not much over four feet tall, and it walked with a hunch making the creature seem even shorter.

The Bat Slave stared at us as it moved without any trace of alarm or accusation in its face. Only an expression of fear. The creature never slowed in his step or altered his course. It just kept walking, watching us out of the corner of its eye, then it hurried along without a word to do whatever it was tasked to do.

I glanced back at the others, and they looked as astounded as I felt.

"Come on," I said. "Next time we might not be so lucky."

We pushed forward, passing arch after arch of the lit plastic shoring, then the shaft opened into a lit cavern. We crept closer, inching our way toward the corner so we could peer inside without being seen. To our surprise, we saw a large communal area full of tables, cots, and chairs. There were several side rooms carved into the walls and additional shafts spidering off the central hub in every direction. More surprising was the fact that the entire place seemed to be empty. There wasn't a single Bat Slave or Unicorn in sight.

"Over there." Dirk pointed to the left toward a spot on the wall. The black soil made everything dark and hard to see, but I could just make out some sort of sealed chamber. The only one apparent in the room.

We hurried forward and found the chamber was indeed a sealed vault with a large viewing window on the side. To our utter astonishment, we saw row after row of the snow globes Buttercup had shown us on the ship. The vault was filled with more Void Prisms than the Dazbog could ever dream of, and they were all locked behind an impenetrable door designed to stop anyone from stealing them.

FIFTEEN

"I'll look around and find something to open it." Dirk jetted away ever optimistic, but Elliot snorted out a defeated laugh.

"That is eight-inch fully encased dirantium. Nothing can penetrate that vault." He had already swung his backpack off and rummaged around for something inside. "I doubt I can crack the lock, but I can try. Either way I don't think we should stay for more than a few minutes."

I nodded as he pulled out a tablet, held it near the electronic lock and started punching something on the screen.

"Maybe we can find a Void Prism somewhere else." I turned to look at Lois. She had her face pasted to the clear viewing window. "I mean they don't make them in there, right? Maybe they have some unfinished prisms or a few that were completed in a work area."

I turned my head to peer through the window as well, staring at the rows of perfectly placed globes just out of our grasp.

"If there were, it would take us forever to find them in this maze." Lois sounded hollow and defeated through her respirator. "Considering how well they have these things secured, I doubt they build them in a tool shed. The production area will be locked down just as tight."

Twitch chittered on my shoulder and reached out to put his tiny hand on the window as well.

"Yeah buddy. You're an amazing thief, but I don't think even you can get in there." I stared into the vault, agonizing over the wealth of swirling globes just out of our reach. "If only we had a way in. I can't believe we didn't consider something like this. I'll bet Buttercup could have fabricated something to ..."

I stopped talking when a light brightened the tunnel, then a soft pop vibrated the air around us. Lois and I looked at each other the moment the familiar sound hit our ears. It was Bubbles. She had folded out of her safe space in my carrier backpack to ... well that was the question. Where could she have gone? The reason I brought her with us was because whenever I left her behind, she would fold away and pop into existence right in front of my face. Almost always at the worst possible time.

The realization of what just happened horrified me beyond any fear I had ever experienced in my life. My stomach dropped into my feet and I held my breath as I scanned the room, waiting ... hoping Bubbles would pop back in close enough to catch her.

When Lois let out a little scream, I jerked my head in her direction. She had her eyes on the vault. I followed her terrified gaze and there sat Bubbles, front and center on the top shelf amidst rows and rows of Void Prisms.

I froze. "This is bad."

Lois spun an angry glare in my direction. "I told you something like this would happen." Her voice was somewhere between panic and scolding.

"Is this really the time for I told you so?" I looked all around the frame of the window for another way in. "How are we going to get her out of there?"

Bubbles smiled and bounced on her tiny little tentacles, nearly toppling one of the snow globes to the floor. I had no idea what would happen if one ... or many of them fell and broke on the ground, but I had to assume it would be the opposite of anything good.

I grabbed Elliot by his coat and shook him so hard he almost dropped his tablet. "You have to get us in there right now. She's going to knock over the globes. We can't leave her here for the Unicorns. Open the door, now!"

It took a moment for me to realize Lois had her arms around my waist trying to pull me away from the very terrified looking Dazbog. When I let go, he fell to the ground and skittered backward to escape my frenzied pleas.

"He can't get in if you're shaking him like that." Lois pulled me back and shoved me against the wall on the far side of the window. "You're making too much noise," she hissed. "What are you trying to do? Make *sure* the Unicorns hear us?"

"No." I blinked. "I'm sorry. I just ..." I looked at Elliot. "Please."

He stared back at me, not in fear, but hopelessness. Then Dirk charged between us and smashed into the window with a four-foot metal pipe.

The sound echoed through the cavern like a sledgehammer on steel. It rang out high and loud and did absolutely nothing to the vault. He stared at it in disbelief, unable to compute the fact that his brawn had failed him. He drew back and hit it again and again and again. The sound rang out like an alarm bell. He was so determined it took both Lois and I to wrestle him out of range for another swing.

"Have you lost your mind?" I all but screamed in his face. "What did you think you would do, break into the impenetrable vault with your pipe? That is not a glass window. Even if it was, Bubbles is in there. You could have killed her."

Dirk let the pipe drop to his side, no longer fighting us for another shot at the vault. "I thought ..."

I spun around toward Elliot. "You have to open that thing. Can you do it?"

Elliot stared at me for a moment then scrambled to his feet and nodded. "I will try."

All our hopes hung on the little Dazbog's brainpower and his touchscreen tablet. He started tapping the screen as we watched in anticipation, then a sound came echoing along the cavern walls. If we were on the prairies of eastern Colorado, I would have told you cowboys were on their way, riding their horses hard for a roundup. Here the stomping hooves and snorting breaths could mean only one thing. The Unicorns were back, and we were trapped deep in their caves with nowhere to run.

SIXTEEN

L ois pulled at my arm, jerking me to the side, but I refused
to budge. I couldn't tear my eyes away from Bubbles as
she rocked back and forth, her little mouth smiling as bioluminescent light danced across her skin. Dirk and Elliot had scrambled away. Even Twitch had leapt off my shoulder and taken to
camouflage for escape, but I could not bring myself to leave.
Bubbles was an innocent infant. She had no idea the danger
she was in. To her this was all a game. She could not imagine
the horrors trampling through the tunnels much less the consequences of being found.

"Ben, we have to go." Lois half pleaded, half ordered as she
continued to pull my arm. "We can't help her if we're dead."

That thought pierced through my dread and panic. Lois
was right. As bad as things were, it would do no good to offer
ourselves on a silver platter to the Unicorns. A fighting chance
was better than no chance at all.

I put my hand on the window, then let Lois lead me away. I
had just enough time to see Bubbles' mischievous smile turn
down in shock and betrayal. Her eyes went wide and watery as

if she were about to cry and my chest wound itself into an aching ball of guilt. It was all I could do to stop myself from going back to the window, but If I did, I would be dead.

I staggered behind Lois as she led me around what looked like a huge generator set into the wall a few feet away from the vault. Maintenance access had been dug all around the unit so there was plenty of room for us to fit behind it without being seen. Getting out would be a different story.

"What are we going to do?" I held my palms to my temples, shaking my head in disbelief. "We can't leave her in there. We can't ..."

Dirk grabbed hold of my jacket and jerked me down to face him as he crouched near to the ground. He was much, *much* stronger than Lois, and I found resisting him like resisting the pull of a falling ship anchor.

"Get it together," he said. "We still need to open that vault, and I can't do it if you're back here blubbering."

I lowered my hands and took a breath. I didn't know if he was more interested in saving Bubbles or retrieving a Void Prism. Either way, he was right. We needed a plan, and we needed it fast.

The sound of the hoofbeats grew louder and I could tell they were through the tunnel and into the large communal cavern. The wild chaotic cadence never stopped until they were past our position, then they all skidded to a halt and my gut twisted into knots.

"There is something in the vault!" The voice was deep and resonant and from the sound of their hoofbeats I had to assume there were more than two of them. Probably five or six. Way too many for us to take on in a fight with no weapons other than my revolver. Even with the element of surprise, I could never take them all down before one of them got a shot at us.

"You four head down and secure the mine. Help the others confine the slaves until we find out who is responsible for the attack outside. I'll take care of this pest."

One Unicorn would be much easier to deal with than five. Unfortunately, it sounded like the straggler was on his way into the vault to get Bubbles. If we could wait long enough for the others to move out of sight ...

I pulled Lois, Dirk and Elliot in close so I could talk without being heard over the low drone of the generator.

"Lois, get everyone back to Buttercup. If I'm not with you in fifteen minutes, leave without me. You'll have to find another way to finish the mission."

"Another way?" Lois shout-whispered. "There is no other way. And what are you planning to do?"

"I have to save Bubbles, or at least try. As soon as that Unicorn opens the vault door, I'm going to rush him. I should be able to stun him with my revolver before he brains me with that mace. I'll be right behind you, promise."

I offered her a weak smile then turned and prepared myself to run.

She grabbed my arm, preventing me from getting more than a few inches. "And what if you aren't? What am I supposed to do? Go on traveling the universe all by myself? I don't think so."

"I'm going with you." Dirk made his announcement so loud I feared the Unicorn might hear him. I pressed a finger to my lips trying to quiet everyone down. Our window of opportunity was closing. If we wanted to make a move, we had to do it now.

"Fine. Whatever. Let's just go."

"You're all idiots." Elliot had his head down, digging in his backpack looking for something deep within its recesses. "Give me a second and I will provide a distraction."

"No." Dirk turned a furious glare in his direction. "None of your ridiculous contraptions. Go with Lois. Ben and I will catch up to you when we have the prism."

"And Bubbles," I amended.

"And Bubbles," he agreed.

Elliot kept rummaging but there was no time to argue.

I shook my head and turned to Lois. "This is our only shot. We have to try."

Lois nodded. "Agreed, but we're going to be right here. There is no way I'm leaving you. Besides, who's going to pull your bacon out of the pan when you get caught."

That brought a smile to my lips. "I really miss bacon."

Lois smiled back. "Hurry up before I change my mind."

I nodded and looked at Dirk. Without warning, he shot past me to the edge of the recess, peeked around the corner then scrambled forward.

"Come on, work!" Elliot fumbled with something in his hands, but I didn't have time to see what it was.

Dirk was gone, and if I wanted to keep up with him, I needed to go too. I didn't bother looking around the corner. I just scurried out and scrambled all the way toward the vault to crouch with Dirk under the window. He pointed inside and nodded toward the open door. The Unicorn was already in, but I didn't hear any commotion. Maybe Bubbles had sensed the danger and folded to the ship. Almost anywhere would be better than here.

Dirk crawled forward to the edge of the door. I wanted to tell Dirk to fall back. We would have a much better chance if I went in first to stun the Unicorn with my revolver, but he seemed intent on duking it out hand to hand. A moronic plan even by my standards, considering the size and strength of the Unicorns and volatile nature of the Void Prisms inside the vault. Dirk still had a ways to go with that impulse control problem of his. Maybe I could get a shot off once he cleared the door.

I reached for the holster on my hip, ready to draw my revolver when a familiar light bloomed before my eyes. I released the butt of my gun and held out my hands in time for Bubbles to drop out of thin air into my grasp. Relief washed through me as I pulled the little Viraquin close to my chest, hugging her tight. Tears threatened to well into my eyes. I was so happy to see her, and at the same time I wanted to yell at her for being so irresponsible. When I peered down at her little face, fear and relief hid within her innocent features. It seemed she realized what sort of trouble she had gotten herself into and she was glad to be with me again.

I let out a breath and looked up to see Dirk creep into the opening of the vault door. I reached out to grab him, but as I did something else began to announce its existence behind us. I turned to see something that resembled a toy dog, running and spinning in little circles on the sandy floor. Running wasn't entirely accurate. Its legs were attached to wild spinning wheels and the metal inner structure seemed to be covered with the gruesome remnants of a stuffed animal hide. The whole thing was glued on in a crooked patchy mess and the little robot barked more like a fire alarm than a dog.

I jerked my head toward the window and saw that the Unicorn had its huge gorilla hands pressed to the clear pane, looking out at the shrieking, spinning catastrophe. The moment I moved, his eyes went down to me. We stared at each other, shocked by the spectacle, then we both shot toward the door.

SEVENTEEN

We moved at the same time, but the Unicorn had to dodge around the shelves inside the vault. I was already crouched close to the ground, ready to spring. I launched myself at Dirk, who had turned to stare wide-eyed at the shrieking dog-tastrophy, and shouldered him away from the door. With Bubbles tucked under my right arm, I reached out with my left and slammed the door closed a millisecond before the Unicorn got there. If I had misjudged my leap by an inch, we would have been dead.

I landed hard on my shoulder but managed to twist and avoid crushing Bubbles under my weight. Once I stopped skidding across the sand I sat up with a groan and struggled to my knees. For the first time, Bubbles did not look quite so giggly and carefree. I could see concern in her eyes. I felt all at once heartbroken and glad to see that she understood. Maybe not every detail, but she knew this had gone wrong and this time her hijinks had put her ... all of us in danger. At least it was a start.

A pair of hands hauled me up by my shoulders before I had

a chance to stand on my own. "Do you have any idea what you've done?"

I twisted around toward a red-faced Dirk who had one of his fists wrapped in my coat.

"We have no way into that vault. We can't get to the Void Prisms."

The Unicorn beat at the window with his fists. Spit and foam spewed from his mouth as he screamed what I'm sure were obscenities at us through the soundproofed wall. These guys were terrifying on a good day. When they got angry, they became an absolute nightmare. Being stuck between the furious Unicorn and a furious Dirk was not the most comfortable place to be.

"I had no choice," I said, trying to pull out of his grip without any success. "It was either shut the door or become a Unicorn shish kabob. That barking bag of bolts called him right out to us."

We both turned to look at the dog-trocity. In all the excitement I hadn't even noticed the thing had stopped shrieking and spinning.

Realization dawned in Dirk's eyes, and he jerked his head toward the generator. When I looked as well, I saw Lois standing in front of a very terrified looking Elliot.

"He meant well." Lois had her arms out as if to shield the little Dazbog. "He wanted to help you."

Dirk let go of my coat and stomped toward Lois and Elliot. I spared a glance toward the Unicorn in the vault and saw that he spoke into some sort of communicator on his forearm. This situation was going from bad to worse in a hurry.

"Dirk." I ran around in front of him to block his way, but it was like holding my hand out to stop a bus. "We don't have time for this. The Unicorn is calling for backup. We have to leave."

My words did as much good as my hand. Dirk kept walking, Lois held her ground, and I began to wonder how I could fend off Dirk with Bubbles in my arm. It wasn't until Twitch appeared that anything shook his resolve at all.

He darted between us, catching our attention as we charged forward, then Dirk slowed, then stopped, blinking down at the little Chitterwall. When I dared to look at him as well, I saw that he held something in his hands. It was not quite half the size of his entire body, round and set into a small silver pedestal. Snow swirled around the globe, obscuring the prism inside, but there was no doubt as to what Twitch held in his hand.

"How ..." was all Dirk said, then I reached down and snatched the Void Prism out of Twitch's miraculous hands.

"You thieving little rascal." I laughed. "Did you sneak in there and steal this before I slammed the door?"

Twitch chittered and scurried up my leg to my shoulder.

"Good work buddy. We all owe you a big one."

I held the globe out to Dirk. "Don't we?"

Dirk blinked for a moment then offered a slow nod.

"Good." I turned my gaze to Lois who remained in front of Elliot, not quite ready to give up her defensive stance. "We got what we came for. Let's get out of here before anymore—"

Before I could finish, an energy beam streaked across the chasm and struck the rock to our left. The wall exploded in a spray of black sand, then more energy bolts came lancing in our direction.

We turned to see the contingent of Unicorns returning from the splinter shafts in the mine. Their mace weapons were up and firing as they galloped toward us. Time to run.

EIGHTEEN

With Bubbles in one hand and the globe in the other, I couldn't draw my revolver. I tossed the Void Prism to Dirk and then drew my gun, thumbing the barrel to the red-light setting as I took aim. When I fired, the staccato thump sounded much different from the crackling stun charges I had fired before. These were explosive rounds, and they streaked toward their target like miniature phosphorescent missiles. They struck the top of the tunnel in a flash of concussive force so deep I felt it in my chest. My ears popped and we were all blown back a step as rock and debris rained down on the Unicorns unfortunate enough to be standing in the rearward tunnels.

I paused a moment and stared at my gun.

"Do not fire that weapon inside the mine." Buttercup shouted in my head. "You could bring the entire complex down on top of you, not to mention hundreds of innocent slave miners."

"Now you tell me." I thumbed the cylinder off the explosive-round setting and the lights on the revolver changed momentarily from red to orange before reverting back to the default blue. Buttercup had told me what all the settings and colors meant, but other than the exploding one, I couldn't remember what they were. I hoped this orange setting wouldn't kill us all.

Dirk crouched to pick up the globe from the ground. Either he had missed my toss or dropped it in the explosion. When he didn't dive for cover, I assumed the casing hadn't ruptured and we were okay.

"That cave-in isn't going to hold them for long." I nodded everyone toward the large exit cavity that led to the surface. "We need to get out of—"

More of the deadly red energy bolts shattered rock above our heads, interrupting before I could finish, as four more Unicorns rounded the corner from another shaft.

I raised my revolver and blasted off two rounds. I didn't have time to aim but I hoped my return fire would at least slow them down. As it turned out, aiming was not a prerequisite for this setting. The thump, hiss was similar to the sound of the explosive round, but not as concussive. When I saw the shells curve and track their targets, I all but tripped over my own feet.

The heat seeking projectiles struck two of the Unicorns square in the chest, dropping them before they could take another step and forced the other two into cover.

Lois, Dirk and Elliot were already running, and I paused long enough to let Twitch scurry up to my shoulder before I turned to stay dead on their heels. The Unicorns were not a race of cowards. They would be after us no matter what I threw at them. Best that we stayed ahead of them while we could.

"Buttercup," I sprinted forward keeping Bubbles tucked close to my body as I clutched the revolver in my other hand. I didn't have time to put her in my pack so she would have to ride this one out NFL style. "We're coming out on the run. Is there any way you can meet us at the mine? I don't think we're going to make it to our rendezvous point."

"Affirmative." It was all the response she offered. I hoped it would be enough. We still had to make it outside in order for Buttercup to help us and getting that far would be a problem.

The monumental flaw in our escape plan became evident the moment we stepped into the main tunnel. It was long, wide and open ... too open. There was no cover, no curves or corners to hide behind. This was our only way out, but to get there we would be exposed long enough to rattle a nudist colony.

"We're never going to make it," Lois shrieked as she ran, her voice panicked and breathless.

"Keep running." I turned and fired two more rounds blind to our rear. "We can make it."

When I looked back, I knew we wouldn't. The Unicorns adapted to my heat-seeking rounds faster than I could have imagined. Four of the uni-horned monsters charged into the tunnel behind us carrying large shields followed by six more. The moment they had us in view they began firing.

Glowing red bolts of energy rained in around us, hailing sand and rock onto our heads. The deafening noise of their guns and impacts echoed off the walls. It was so terrifying my first instinct was to dive to the ground and cover my head in a feeble attempt to save myself from the horrifying onslaught. As it turned out, salvation came in a much smaller package.

"I've got this." Elliot had turned and ran headlong into the Unicorns' energy bolt assault. He fumbled, putting on some sort of gold belt, and seemed determined to fall back behind me. "Keep going."

The moment the belt latched, a bright blue light lit up the mine. Elliot had activated a personal energy shield, much like the one Dirk wore on his arm, but this one was bigger ... much bigger. It took up almost half the width of the mineshaft and was at least eight feet in height. Plenty of cover for all of us to make our escape.

"Elliot, you're a genius." I had stopped running to admire his bravery and ingenuity.

"Keep going." He screeched, ignoring my admiration. "The power cell for a shield this large is limited. We only have a few seconds."

I nodded and took up the race to escape. Lois and Dirk had paused ahead as well, but as soon as they saw me running, they ran too. The Unicorns would either have to run us down from behind or find a way to head us off, and considering the head start we now had, I thought both possibilities were unlikely.

We sprinted almost fifty yards before the first energy bolt broke through.

It hit high on the ceiling over my head. I thought the shot skimmed past the top of Elliot's shield but when I looked back, I saw different.

Elliot was on his knees, buckling under the barrage of energy bolts that hit his shield. Apparently, intelligent as he was, Elliot hadn't accounted for the sheer weight of a large, coordinated attack. He did all he could to keep his shield upright, but the Unicorns were smart. They had focused their fire on the top of his shield, levering him downward, so he could no longer run, or even stand.

I skidded to a halt and turned to run toward Elliot. We couldn't leave him. Maybe the two of us could withstand the onslaught together. Even as I thought it, the shield flickered. The power cells were fading. We had only seconds before we were fish in a barrel. As soon as the shield went down, we would be done.

"Hold on Elliot." The voice came from behind me. "I'm coming."

I ran at a full sprint, but Dirk overtook my position to get to Elliot first. Dirk never hesitated as he leapt behind him, activating the bands he wore on his own arm. His shield flared to life and although it was much smaller than Elliot's, it was big enough to protect the two of them.

"Come on." I crouched in front of Elliot, urging him forward, but he would not move. Instead, he clawed at his belt in a desperate attempt to remove it.

"Something's wrong." Lois panted as she ran up behind us, ducking behind Dirk's shield as well. "The belt. It's hurting him."

Elliot nodded emphatically and I noticed he wasn't breathing. His face had turned red and if we didn't do something fast, we'd be carrying Elliot out of here on our shoulders.

"Here they come." Dirk announced. "Is Elliot okay? We need to get him out of here."

I looked up to see the Unicorns advancing behind their own shield wall.

"Here, let me try this." Lois reached into her purse and pulled out a pair of pink-handled scissors. I had my hands full with Bubbles and my revolver so I switched places with her, keeping everyone in line with Dirk's smaller shield, but we couldn't sit there forever.

Even if we got Elliot up and running again, the Unicorns would be able to pick us off one by one. They were closer now and we would be hard to miss. Unless ...

I examined my revolver, remembering one of the other settings. I rotated the barrel turning the indicator lighting to white, then I rose above Dirk's shield and fired.

The effect was immediate. I hit my mark and it stopped

them in their tracks. An armor piercing round penetrated through the shield of the lead Unicorn dropping not only him, but the Unicorn behind him as well.

I rose to shoot again but this time they were ready. They concentrated their fire, making Dirk groan with the effort but I scored another hit, and two more Unicorns went down. With only two shields left they began to fall back, scrambling to maintain their cover fire as they moved.

I glanced down. Elliot was breathing, and his gold belt lay on the ground. So were Lois' scissors. They were now a bent-up ruin, but they had done their job.

"Are we good?"

Lois laid a hand on Elliot's shoulder, and he nodded. He rose to his feet and together, we retreated up the tunnel toward our escape. I continued to fire at the Unicorn's line, but they had pulled back to a safer distance. Harder for me to hit them, but harder for them to hit us as well.

We were almost home free when Elliot stumbled, holding his side where the belt had cinched around his body.

I stepped to the side avoiding him and so did Lois, but Dirk walked backward, holding his shield and didn't see him.

"Look out!" Lois tried to warn him, but it was too late. Dirk tripped over Elliot's body and sprawled to the ground.

Dirk's shield blinked twice and then went out. A line of the Unicorn's red energy bolts tore along the sand and struck Dirk's prostrate body.

"No!" Elliot shouted and scrambled toward Dirk. I fired my revolver again and again. Buttercup told me it had a limited power supply, so I had been conservative with my shots. Now I laid down fire without regard to location or limits. I pulled the trigger again and again, doing my best to keep the Unicorns on their heels. If we didn't get out now, we weren't going to get out at all.

"How is he?" I spared a glance at Dirk and saw Elliot and Lois holding their hands to his chest. Bubbles still rode in my arm and Twitch clutched my shoulder, but at least we were all together.

"I could be better, but I'm alive."

The sound of Dirk's voice sent a wave of relief over me.

"Can you walk?"

"I'll carry him if I have to." A moment ago, Elliot was barely able to stand, now he was ready to throw Dirk over his shoulder Forest Gump style and run him all the way to the ship. Adrenaline. What a wonderful thing.

"We'll get him going." Lois was already helping Dirk to his feet. He had a hand to his chest, holding Lois' scarf to his wound. Elliot propped himself under Dirk's other arm and together they started moving.

I switched my revolver to heat seeker mode and fired several shots over the Unicorn's heads. We had a little elevation on them now and I hoped the projectiles would curve down and find their target. Five shots missed, but the sixth found its mark, taking one of the rear most Unicorns. That was enough to send them back the way they came. The five remaining Unicorns turned to retreat into the mine, leaving us a clear path to our escape.

"Keep going." I jogged backward, not willing to give up our flank in case the Unicorns decided to reappear. "Buttercup said she would meet us outside."

Natural light began to bathe my back and I knew we were close. We kept running, Lois and Elliot all but carried Dirk while I acted as security. The feeling of vitality and freedom overwhelmed me the moment we broke out of the cave. Even though we were on a dead, scorching planet with pelting black sand, being out of those mines felt like utter redemption.

I shielded Bubbles the best I could from the elements while Lois and Elliot kept their heads down and continued to run. I slowed slightly, scanning the desolate landscape. "Buttercup, where are you?"

No response.

"Where is she?" Lois shouted over the wind, sounding angry, panicked and exhausted.

I spun all around, sand pelting me from every side as I hurried farther from the mine. "Buttercup. We need you. There are Unicorns on our tail."

Still nothing.

Lois and Elliot stopped running. When I caught up, I stopped too. There was no place left to run. Out here it was all scorching sand and violet colored lava flows. If the Unicorns didn't kill us, the planet would. At least we had a fighting chance against the Unicorns.

Then everything around us began to move. Unicorns emerged from dunes and rocks and from behind machinery. Even the Unicorns from the mine had reversed their retreat, heading us off at the mouth of the cave as well. There had to be more than a hundred of the monstrous looking giants, and they were all pointing their energy maces right at us.

NINETEEN

W e all threw our hands into the air. Well, almost all of us. I dropped my revolver and raised one hand. I had Bubbles in the other. Lois and Elliot both raised one hand as well, the other supporting Dirk's listless form. I saw Twitch raise his little arms into the air, but he disappeared almost as fast, camouflaging himself from view.

"Buttercup." I ground the word through my teeth. "We are going to die if you don't do something right this second."

Lois looked at me and I stared back at her.

"Maybe something happened to her," Lois said. "The planetary defense systems could have activated, or maybe the Unicorns got to her."

I shook my head. Buttercup and I shared a neural link. It was an advanced intelligence system that allowed Buttercup to utilize my biological synapses, but it also offered us a sort of connection. I did not share her thoughts or know her exact location, but I did know when something was wrong. If she was in trouble, I would be in trouble too, and so far, I felt nothing that told me Buttercup was anything but late to the party.

I turned my attention to a Unicorn who slowly made his way forward from the mine through the wind and swirling sand. He was the only one *not* aiming his mace in our direction. Instead, he smacked it again and again in the palm of his hairy gorilla hand.

"Listen." I smiled, lowering my hand in front of me to show the oncoming Unicorn my empty palm. "I'm sure we can talk this out. We're all on the same team here."

Lois looked at me. "What?"

I shrugged. "I don't know what else to say. This guy is about to bash our heads in. What do you suggest? Unicorns suck?"

The Unicorns had begun to chant. Well, not so much chant, but grunt through their noses. It was a deep, disturbing rhythmic sound. Slow and purposeful, timed to coincide with each of the oncoming Unicorn's steps.

Lois turned toward him. "He was kidding about the Unicorns suck thing. We love unicorns on Earth. They're soft and fluffy and shoot rainbows out of ... everyone wants a unicorn. We give them to our children."

"I'm not so sure your argument is impressing him." I watched the menacing figure that in no way resembled the unicorns we were accustomed to on Earth.

"It's better than Unicorns suck."

The rhythmic grunts got faster as the Unicorn approached. When he was right in front of us, he stood, smacking his hand with his mace, staring down at us without expression.

I dropped my arm to my side and turned slightly to angle Bubbles away from him. "If you're going to do something, do it, but don't just stand there and smell bad."

That drew the tiniest of smiles from the Unicorn. He raised his mace high over his head. I closed my eyes not wanting to see the blow coming. The worst thing wasn't me, but everyone else.

Bubbles and Twitch. What would happen to them? I could only hope Bubbles would fold away to somewhere safe, but Twitch would have to figure out a way to live here. He was a survivor though. The little Chitterwall had already scampered to safety. He would be fine. Lois would not, nor would Elliot and Dirk. They would suffer the same fate as me. I just hoped it would be quick. For all our sakes.

I waited for the blow to come, then there was a familiar whump and a momentary heat flashed against my face. When I opened my eyes there was nothing left of the Unicorn but two hooves in the sand, supporting short stubs where the legs had been.

Lois stared at the gruesome sight then let out a scream. "What was that!"

I just smiled, then Buttercup materialized on a dune to our left.

"Time to go." I snatched my revolver off the ground as Buttercup unleashed hell upon the Unicorns. Green energy bolts exploded into the sand and rocks forcing them to take cover. They did their best to return fire, but hand blasters did little to damage Buttercup's tough hull.

I fired my revolver at the Unicorns still standing near the mine, but they had retreated inside. At least that meant five less Unicorns to fire at us. Buttercup unleashed against the Unicorns without restraint. Blasts from her energy weapons threw around so much sand I could no longer tell where the Unicorns were, so I just ran instead.

Lois and Elliot scrambled up Buttercup's ramp to safety with Dirk. Now it was my turn. I sprinted toward the open ramp, then a figure emerged out of a cloud of swirling sand halting my escape. I drew my revolver, ready to fire, but held back at the last moment. This was no Unicorn. It wasn't one of the slaves either. This creature was something else entirely.

The tall, slender figure had humanoid body features, but the graceful neck stretched up into the head of a sharp-nosed canine. Its ears stood high on its head and the piercing ice-white eyes contrasted with the creature's ebony black skin. The beige robes it wore completed the image, unmistakably Egyptian. Anubis, if memory served, and spot on in its representation.

"Please." The creature had a soft female voice. "Help me. The Unicorns have taken me captive. I need help."

She staggered toward me, one hand clutched to her side, heedless of my revolver. Violet colored blood seeped through her fingers. She was injured, and for the life of me I didn't know what to do.

She could be telling the truth, or she could be an enemy trying to get past our defenses. I had no idea which one.

She fell to her knees a few feet from where I stood. Not because she was begging, but because she couldn't seem to run any further. "I can help you. The planetary defense systems. You will not be able to escape orbit unless they are disabled. I know the codes."

I stared at her, still not knowing whether to believe her.

"Ben, we have to go."

It was Buttercup. She broke in over our internal communications system as she continued to lay down fire.

"The Unicorns are bringing heavy artillery in from the mine. Their hand blasters are not a problem, but I do not want to be here when they establish real weapons."

"Okay."

I paused for another second, then turned away from the creature kneeling on the ground. It was too big of a chance. If she were an enemy, she could ... what? I stopped. She wasn't armed and she was hurt. Could I leave someone like that lying in the sand?

I sighed and turned to the Anubis creature.

"You better be worth it, Lady." I holstered my revolver and knelt beside her so she could get an arm over my shoulder. With Bubbles cradled in my arm, I couldn't help much but at least I could act as a crutch. She was a foot taller than me, but she slumped over, leaning her slender weight into me. "I have a feeling I'm not going to hear the end of this one."

TWENTY

I walked onto the bridge with our new passenger expecting to face dismay, disbelief, maybe a little opposition. The moment I laid eyes on Elliot, I knew it would be much, much worse.

I spun to the side, struggling to put myself between our new guest and the little charging Dazbog. I had Bubbles in one hand and the Anubis occupied the other, so all I could do was run bodily interference.

"Where did you find one of them?" Elliot's voice was full of more hatred and fury than I ever thought possible. "I should have guessed you would be working side by side with those monsters."

I did my best to push him away with my foot to stop the frenzied assault. "Hold on a second. She said the planetary defense systems were still active. If that's true, we're never going to make it off this rock in one piece without her help."

The Anubis alien hung on me with almost all her weight now. If she wasn't unconscious now, she would be in a moment.

Elliot stopped trying to get around me, but he remained a few inches away, huffing loud angry breaths through his nose.

"Buttercup, Lois, a little help here."

"I am afraid Ben is correct in his assessment. I was barely able to override the surface defenses in time to assist with your Unicorn encounter. If I had decloaked any sooner, I would have brought down more than the wrath of a few insignificant hand blasters."

"Insignificant ..." I started to say, then got back on track. "What about the orbital defense systems?"

"The orbital defense systems are now on alert and aware of my presence. They will be impossible to override without a key code."

I looked to Elliot. He still wouldn't give any ground, but he didn't seem quite so determined in his assault either.

"Back off or you can kiss this ship and everyone on it good-bye. She's getting heavy and I don't know how much longer I can hold her this way."

"Elliot." Lois scolded. "Forget about that for a minute and help me over here." She knelt next to Dirk, pressing a field dressing to his chest. Elliot glared at me for a half a second longer, then scurried back to his friend, all hate and malice gone from his face.

"Come on." I wasted no time walking our new guest to Elliot's chair. He would not be happy about that either, but it was the closest one, and right now, every moment counted. "Stay with me a few more seconds."

I hurried to put Bubbles in my chair and Twitch glided in to meet us. "Glad to see you little buddy. I was worried about you back there."

Twitch chittered and turned his attention to Bubbles. They greeted each other with a sort of solemn gratitude and Twitch soothed Bubbles with a kind hand. I could tell they were both glad to see each other.

"Buttercup, can you access the orbital defense system?"

"Yes, but without a code I cannot—"

I held up my hand to stop her and rushed around to crouch in front of the Anubis. "Time to earn your passage. If you don't want to die right now, we need that code."

The Anubis uttered something my translator did not understand. Maybe it was a letter or number. She whispered four more characters, each one fainter and further apart than the last.

"One more," Buttercup snapped. "There is a countdown timer. The code must be entered, or the system will lock down."

"Come on." I gave her a gentle tap on the cheek, but she just murmured something unintelligible. I glanced at Lois and Elliot. They were both busy with Dirk, so I reached back and persuaded her a little harder.

The Anubis jolted awake for a moment, and I grabbed her by the shoulders. "The last character in the code. What is it?"

She began to fade and for a moment I thought she might not have it in her, but at the last second, she murmured something.

"That's it!" Buttercup announced. "The system is deactivated. We need to escape before the Unicorns reboot. I doubt they will have the same password next time."

"Get us out of here!" I all but shouted the order, then turned my attention to our new guest. She was injured and unconscious. I was a nurse, but human biology was a lot different from ... whatever she was. I would just have to try to stop the bleeding and hope it was not as bad as it looked.

I hurried to the spot where Lois and Elliot tended to Dirk.

They had his head propped on a pad and Elliot clutched Dirk's hand in his own.

"This is all my fault. I'm so sorry." He was on the verge of tears as he stared down at his friend. "You were right. My contraptions are terrible. All they do is get people hurt. If you come out of this, I promise never to use any of my inventions again."

"Hey." I put a hand on his shoulder and looked at Lois. She had done a good job of patching Dirk up, but like my patient, there wasn't much more to do than stop the bleeding and hope for the best. "This was not your fault."

Lois put a hand on his leg as well. "Ben's right. You didn't do this. The Unicorns did. Don't beat yourself up. It could have happened to any one of us."

"But it happened to him ... because of me."

I wanted to say more but I needed to return to my patient in the chair.

"Can I have a couple of those dressings?" I pointed at the case Lois had retrieved from the cargo bay. We kept two casualty kits for these sorts of emergencies. I had hoped we would never have to use them.

Lois reached into the case and handed me two of the paper wrapped packages. Elliot glanced at me with disdain in his eyes but didn't say anything else. We would have to work out the peace treaty later. For now, I needed to make sure no one died.

I hurried to the Anubis and peeled back a section of her robes to expose the jagged slice on her skin. It didn't appear to go deep enough to hit anything vital, but it was still a serious wound. At least the bleeding had slowed. If I patched her up, she might be okay.

I cleaned and dressed the ugly laceration then secured the whole thing with several wraps around her waist to maintain pressure. Without some sort of trained alien medical staff, it was all I could do.

"How is Dirk doing over there?" I looked at Lois and she shrugged.

"He seems to be breathing okay. I don't really know how to tell."

"His vital signs are stable," Buttercup said. "I will be able to monitor him as long as he is in physical contact with my hull."

My eyebrows went up. "Great. What about her?"

I indicated the Anubis alien sitting unconscious in front of me.

"She is one of the Cur."

I thought Buttercup's voice sounded a little less hospitable. "My database is less extensive on her race. From what I can surmise she is also stable. I do not believe her injuries are in danger of being fatal at this time. She will likely wake up on her own and attempt to kill us all."

I backed away from her before I realized what I was doing. "Wait, what? We helped her."

"I am making an assumption based purely on her association with the Unicorns and the Cur's current conflict with the Dazbog. She will consider herself a prisoner of war. She will either try to escape or attempt to capture the ship by force. As there is no way to escape, there is only one other choice."

"There are more choices than that," Lois scoffed. "She could find a way to self-destruct the ship and kill everyone on board including herself in an act of rebellion."

I gawked at her.

"I stand corrected," Buttercup said. "That would constitute an alternate choice."

"She's not going to kill us." I annunciated each word for effect.

Lois let out a self-satisfied chuckle. "Maybe everyone should relax, and when they wake up and feel better, we can talk things through."

Elliot let out his own scoff, but I didn't rise to the bait.

"Excellent," I said. "In the meantime, is there a medical facility within range? Someone who might be able to help these two better than we can?"

"I am afraid the local *space hospital* is out of our reach."

The way she said space hospital made me think it wasn't a thing, but I refused to ask.

"My Warpstream drive remains offline and though damage repairs from the asteroid field are progressing, our starboard engine is only operating at seventy percent. Hull damage to the rear of the ship is rather extensive as well. Currently, I am proceeding away from the Unicorn's planet at my maximum velocity in the event that they have the ability to launch an interstellar craft to pursue us."

"That's a horrifying thought." Lois stood and walked over to me. I got to my feet as well, but Elliot remained by Dirk's side. "How long before we'll be able to jump to Warpstream?"

"No time soon, I am afraid. Damage was extensive and our efforts on the planet cut into my power resources used for repair."

"We're never going to get back to Earth in time for Christmas." Lois peered at me, her eyes full of defeat and desperation.

"Never say never." I smiled and looked over at Bubbles. "There's always hope."

Bubbles cooed, seeming a little less playful than usual.

"You know I love Bubbles too." Lois peered down at her as well, but her expression was full of frustration and concern. "But she could have really gotten hurt in there, or worse."

I lost my smile thinking of the possibilities and sighed. "I don't know what you want me to do. Look at her. She's a baby. If a human baby kept crawling out of her crib, would you punish her?"

Lois groaned, conceding my point. "No, but a human baby doesn't have this sort of power either. We have to do something, or she's going to get hurt, or hurt all of us." Her voice rose in volume with every word, and the watery-eyed expression of concern on Bubbles' little face grew deeper.

"I understand your point." I spoke through my teeth, trying to force a smile for Bubbles' sake. "You've mentioned it a thousand times. You still can't punish a baby to make her understand what she's doing is dangerous. Especially when she can warp us all into oblivion if she gets angry."

Lois turned toward me, making no effort to mask her anger. "So, we just let her continue? Let her fold us wherever she likes? What happens the next time she pops herself into the middle of a bunch of monsters? Are you going to dive in and save her? Keep saving her until you're dead ... we're all dead?"

"Yeah." I nodded. "I will keep on saving her, and I will save you too. That's what we do. We look out for each other even when we do something stupid. I know we can't go on like this, but we're not going to punish her when she has no idea why she is being punished. In her eyes we would be attacking her for no reason. Either we find another way, or we cope with what we have. That's the best we can do."

Lois bared her teeth, ready to shout a reply, but a squeak of sorrow escaped Bubbles' little mouth, melting the both of us into instant regret.

"Oh, it's okay." Lois reacted first, maybe because she was more vocal and felt the most guilt for upsetting her. She crouched in front of the chair and stroked Bubbles' smooth little head. "Ben and I are just talking. Don't worry about his dumb old angry face."

I coughed out a laugh. "My dumb old face? You were the one—"

Before I could finish, our Cur guest coughed, gasped in a deep breath then opened her eyes. The haunting white color of her stare did nothing to improve her intimidating appearance.

She stiffened in alarm at first, but when she looked at me, then Lois, she relaxed back into her chair. "Thank you." The words came out almost as a breathless whisper. She examined her side and saw my handywork, then touched the bandages and winced.

"You may want to take it easy for a while." I extended a hand to stop her from moving too much. "That gash is pretty bad."

She nodded and settled in again. "How, may I ask, did you find yourselves on that planet? To my knowledge there are few who know it exists."

"We were there to take what was rightfully ours." Elliot snapped at her without moving from his position. He had been so quiet I almost forgot he was there.

The Cur couldn't see him from where she sat, so she moved slowly to peer around the back of the chair. The moment she laid eyes on Elliot and Dirk her demeanor changed.

She shrieked in horror and fell onto the floor, clutching her side as she dragged herself away from them. She didn't stop until she was on the far side of the bridge, pressed against the wall, shuddering in terror.

"You are allied with the destroyers?" Her voice was high and panicked. "What have I done? I should have remained a captive of the Unicorns."

TWENTY-ONE

"Destroyers?" I held my hands in front of me as I inched my way in her direction. "Take it easy. There are no destroyers here."

The Cur would not take her eyes off Elliot and Dirk, even though Dirk was unconscious, and Elliot had his back to her, obviously more concerned about his fallen companion than her.

Lois stood and crept beside me to block The Cur's line of sight, forcing those haunting white eyes up to her. "Maybe we should start with your name. I'm Lois and this is Ben. They are Elliot and Dirk and the voice you hear over the speakers is Buttercup."

I felt a pang of protectiveness when Lois mentioned her name. Buttercup's introduction was usually met with gasps of disgust and some comment about her being an abomination due to her illegal sentient nature, but this time the Cur seemed to take it in stride, either because it was no surprise, or because she was just too frightened to care.

"May we know your name?" I spoke in the gentlest of

voices, but she flinched when her eyes flicked to me. After a second of wild-eyed staring, she said, "Oola. Oola Targreth."

"Oola. That's a beautiful name," Lois soothed. "I can promise you no one is going to hurt you here. You have nothing to fear."

"Ha." Oola tilted her head so she could get an eye on Elliot again as if she thought maybe he was trying to sneak up on her. "The destroyers know nothing of peace. They know only how to spread turmoil and sadness."

"Turmoil and sadness?" Elliot spit the words out in angry shouts. "We spread light and life. We help those who would otherwise perish. You're the one hiding behind those monsters back on that planet. You hoard your prisms like a starving dog, hiding them away, there in your dark corner of the universe, but that's all about to change. As soon as I get home, I'll tell the Dazbog where you are, and they will end your tyranny."

"Tyranny?" Oola forced herself to her feet, but she leaned against the wall, looking as if she didn't have the strength to stand on her own. Just the same, I moved between her and the Dazbog sitting on the ground.

"Take it easy," I said. "We're all friends here."

"I am no friend of the Dazbog." She sneered, but on her it looked more like a snarl. "And the only tyranny that needs to end is your own."

She turned her eyes to Lois and I, and some of the anger melted out of her eyes.

"Do you have any idea who you have allied with? The Dazbog play God in the universe, indiscriminately choosing which race, which planets are worthy of their attention. Who will live or die. I have witnessed the systems who suffer due to overpopulation and famine where the Dazbog advanced a race beyond its natural limits. The devastation of a society lifted to enlightenment despite their inability to evolve beyond their violent natures. The Scavid are now the scourge of the universe, and a product of the Dazbog's thoughtless actions."

That was enough to set me back a step. Were the Dazbog responsible for creating the Scavid? The most dangerous and hated artificially intelligent species in the universe? The implications of such an accusation were staggering.

"He speaks of tyranny, but we're the only thing standing between them and utter chaos. In the beginning, we agreed to supply the Void Prisms thinking the Dazbog had a noble cause. They returned our generosity by spreading hardship and imbalance in every galaxy. We only wish for a natural progression of life without artificial advancement. The universe will take care of itself if only it is allowed to."

I stared at Oola, not knowing what to say. Lois seemed as stunned as I was, and to make matters worse, Elliot had not denied any of it.

I turned to see if he was shaking his head, staring in disbelief, anything that would lead me to believe what Oola said was wrong, but Elliot just sat with his back to us, holding Dirk's hand, acting as if we weren't there.

Suddenly I understood why the Dazbog and the Cur were at war. On one side, the Cur believed the universe was being perverted and twisted into something it should never have been. On the other, the Dazbog believed they brought hope and the prospect of a future where otherwise there might not be one. Both sides had their merits and monumental drawbacks. I had no idea what to do or which way to turn. How could I choose when neither of them was right ... and yet they both were.

"Elevated heart rates and breathing combined with an irritating silence would indicates that you and Lois are in a state of distress over this odd conundrum." Buttercup's voice came so unexpected it made us all jump. "If I may make a suggestion, the fate of the Cur and the Dazbog will likely not be solved by the dizzying intellect of two humans in the next few moments. In the meantime, I suggest you carry on as tradition dictates until a mutual solution is reached between these warring factions."

I nodded, giving Oola an apologetic look, then turned my eyes to Lois. "Buttercup's right. We can't pump the breaks now, not when it would mean the extinction of all the children on Earth. We should press on, and if we can help them to come to some sort of understanding, all the better."

Lois nodded. "I agree. We only have one problem. We still don't have a way to travel to Earth, so this whole conversation is academic."

"Two problems actually," Elliot said, finding his voice again. "Even if we made it there in time, we have no one to do the job. Thanks to me, your Santa is ..."

Elliot choked up, not quite able to finish the thought.

"That's not true," I said. "We still have a Santa on board. We have you."

Elliot coughed out a laugh. "Yeah. I could do it. No problem."

"It's settled then." I smiled as if everything had fallen into place just as I had planned. "All we have to do is get to Earth in time for Christmas."

My eyes turned to Bubbles, who sat on my chair with Twitch. They played the way children do when adults are talking, and they were too bored to listen.

Lois looked at her too, and together we headed over to solve the riddle that would unravel the mystery of Bubbles' space folding impulses.

TWENTY-TWO

"What sort of creature is that?" Oola peered at the chair Bubbles and Twitch occupied.

"This." I patted Twitch on the head, and he immediately turned and scurried up my shoulder to stand tall for his introduction. "This is Twitch. He's a Chitterwall. I guess we neglected to mention him earlier. Sorry about that big guy."

Twitch chittered in response, and I reached up for a tiny fist-bump before turning my innocent expression to Oola again. I knew what she meant, of course. I just wanted to have a little fun.

Lois did not share my enthusiasm for shenanigans and deadpanned a look in my direction before she answered for me.

"This is Bubbles. She is very special, and we are trying to return her to her mother. For now, she's with us."

Lois left it at that. Oola might work out that Bubbles was a Viraquin and, up to now, we had gone to great pains to keep her existence on this ship a secret. We failed miserably at that task, so instead we decided it would be best to go with discretion and keep only necessary people in the know. Like it or not, that included wayward injured hitchhikers who resided in clear view of Bubbles on the bridge.

Oola peered at the little pink Viraquin and Bubbles smiled back, playing a wave of bioluminescent light across her skin. I was sure Oola had more questions, but Lois and I turned in unison, cutting her off before she could ask, and crouched in front of Bubbles on the chair.

"There must be a way to communicate where we want to go." I stroked my fingers over Bubbles' smooth head and smiled at her. I had become more than a little attached to our adorable infant, and the thought of giving her up to her mother already tugged at my heart.

"What happened in the mine?" Lois leaned her elbow on the chair and looked at Bubbles as well. "Try to remember everything. What you felt, how you stood, what you thought about ..."

"We stood in front of the window looking in. I had my hands on the glass like this." I held my hands up by way of example. "And I wondered how we were going to steal one of the Void Prisms."

"That's it? You thought about how to steal a Prism?"

I shrugged. "I wanted to get into the vault. But that's pretty much the same thing."

"That is not the same thing. You wanted in and she went in." Lois paused, looking deep in thought. "Maybe that's it. Maybe we have to picture where we want to go, and she takes us there."

"That makes sense, but I feel like we tried that. Buttercup brought up images of the fairies ... er, Peeri and that seemed to work but then we tried other images and Bubbles had no interest."

Lois held out a hand looking a little alarmed. "Don't think about the Peeri. Think about Earth. Nothing else."

"Right, sorry." I nodded. "I guess we can see what happens this time." I turned my head toward the forward viewscreen and nodded at the Buttercup's sine wave.

"Can you bring up some images of Earth? Maybe some stuff that can jog our memories and show Bubbles some visual cues?"

Still photos began to scroll on the screen showing all manner of locations and events. We spun Bubbles' chair around so she saw them too. When her eyes rose to the flickering spectacle she rocked back and cooed at the dazzling display.

Lois and I crouched on either side of her chair watching the images as well.

"Try to think of Earth," Lois said. "Concentrate on it as a place you want to go."

I watched the images on the screen scroll by. The Statue of Liberty, Scottish Highlands, Russian architecture. Every image recognizable as a place I had seen on the internet or TV. I hadn't traveled much when I lived on Earth. Something I regretted. I never saw all the things the world had to offer and now I might never see those things again.

As the stock photos scrolled by, I thought more and more and more about home. Then something caught my eye.

"Hold on a sec." I pointed at the screen. "Can you go back a few frames?"

Buttercup complied, and when she got to the correct picture, I held out my hand. "Stop. That's the one."

I smiled as an image of the Buzzard's Roost occupied the screen. I had grown up and lived in a tiny town in Colorado.

There wasn't much to do, but there was one bar where all the locals hung out. The Buzzard's Roost.

"Where did you find that picture?"

"I downloaded it from a set of stock photos pertaining to your hometown," Buttercup answered. "I thought you might like to see them someday."

"You thought right." I chuckled. "I spent many hours sitting at that bar. Isaac was a great friend. He was the bartender and better than any psychologist for talking about your woes. He was always there to lend an ear, a dollar, or a drink. Whatever you needed. I sure wish I could see that guy again."

As I crouched there reminiscing about Isaac and my days at the Buzzard Roost, something began to happen. Light bloomed on the chair to my left and when I looked down, I saw that Bubbles had all but disappeared in the blinding white brilliance. Space around her began to warp, then the warp expanded, growing until we were all sucked into the void with a pop, and we were gone.

TWENTY-THREE

The moment we popped out of the fold, Lois and I both stood and turned our heads toward the front viewscreen. My eyes filled with tears. I was struck by how much I had missed the big, beautiful planet we called Earth. Seeing it on the screen was like reuniting with a long-lost love. Bubbles had come through when we needed her the most. She had brought us home.

I turned to scoop Bubbles out of my chair and lifted her into the air.

"You did it. I'm so pr ...hic ... proud of you." I grumbled at the reappearance of the now predictable hiccups and dreaded taking a breath through my nose. Sure enough, I was hit with a lovely bouquet. This time it was rotting trash. If only we could find a way to fix these side effects.

Even the smell of a city dump couldn't wipe the smile off my face. We were home, and more importantly, we had made it in time for Christmas.

Lois walked over next to me and stroked Bubbles' little head as I held her in my arms. Twitch scurried to the back of my chair and hopped over to my shoulder, not wanting to be left out.

"Excuse me, but can some ... hic ... someone please explain what just happened?" Oola had taken a few steps in our direction, but her features were full of fear and uncertainty.

It was funny how most intelligent species seemed to convey emotion the same way. Given the fact that Oola was an alien being, her expressions could have meant joy or anger, but I had no doubt she was frightened. How could she be anything else? Trapped on a ship with her sworn enemy and a couple of humans who had no business being out here in the first place. And now we had been sucked through an impossible fold in space to a planet billions of lightyears from where we started.

Elliot had been through it once before, so he knew what to expect. He was also preoccupied with Dirk on the floor. Oola, however, seemed on the verge of an all-out panic.

"What sort of creature ... hic ... is that? Where are we? How is ... hic ... that possible?"

Lois held her hands out in a calming gesture. "Take it easy. Everything is ... hic ...okay. Bubbles is very special. She can be a little unpredict ... hic ... unpredictable, but this time she brought us right to where we needed to be. As soon as we ... hic ... complete our mission here, we'll see about getting you home."

Oola had her hand pressed to her side where I had bandaged her wounds. Her eyes were wide with fear at first, but then they softened into that lost sleepy look that meant she was about to pass out.

Lois and I got to her just before her legs betrayed her. With Lois on one side and me on the other, we guided her to the rearward chair where Elliot usually sat. It wasn't easy to juggle her and Bubbles at the same time, but somehow, I managed without dropping either of them.

"You're hurt," I said, keeping one hand on her shoulder and my other around Bubbles, who cooed out a concerned little sound and stared wide-eyed at Oola, pulsing her light in slow relaxing beats. "No one here is going to harm you unless you attack us first. You need to rest."

Lois stood on her other side offering a reassuring smile. Oola looked at me, then to her and nodded in agreement, either out of trust or exhaustion, I wasn't sure which. It didn't matter. The fight had run out of her. She closed her eyes, put her head back and let out a deep sigh.

"Thank you for your kindness. I won't forget this when it's all over."

I didn't like the way that sounded but I decided to let it go and smiled at Lois instead.

"She did it." I bounced Bubbles in my arm, and she responded with a giggle and a little light show along her skin. "I don't understand how, but she got us here."

"I think I understand." Lois kept her eyes on Bubbles, smiling almost as wide as me.

"What?" I shook my head. "We didn't do anything different."

"There was one difference. You."

I glanced at Oola. Her eyes were shut, so I pulled my hand away from her shoulder and let Twitch hop down to curl up on the top of her chair and watch over her. Lois and I walked toward my seat, leaving Oola in peace.

"Me? What did I do? I didn't say anything different than you did."

Lois shook her head. "It's not what you say, it's what you feel. When you have a deep connection to a place or when you have a deep need or desire to be somewhere. Not here." She poked her finger at my head. "But here." Then she poked it into my chest.

"It's more than just thinking about it. We saw dozens of pictures of Earth, so did Bubbles, but it wasn't until you saw the photo of the Buzzard's Roost that you had an emotional connection. She's tuned into you. I don't know how, but she knows what you want; what you really want, not just what you ask for, and tries to provide it."

I looked down at Bubbles and the little Viraquin peered at me, grinning with her adorable little mouth.

"She reads my mind? I'm not sure how I feel about that."

"I do not believe she reads your mind," Buttercup said, breaking into the conversation. "However, I find the more plausible hypothesis even more astounding. She is likely intuiting your desires through the Nexus."

I shook my head. "I thought you said it was impossible for someone to hijack our Nexus connection. If you and I are connected, how can she be connected too?"

"And I thought the Nexus was supposed to be a connection between biological and technological beings?" Lois turned to peer at Buttercup's sine wave on the front viewscreen with me. "Not bio to bio."

"Mostly true statements," Buttercup said. "The Peeri can achieve this sort of connection due to their advanced abilities with the Nexus. I have heard of very few species with this bio-to-bio ability, as you put it, but it is possible. As for making the connection while Ben and I are linked, we are faced with a being we know little about. Bubbles can seem to transcend both."

"It does make sense," Lois said. "She always knows where you are and folds to your location. I think she has imprinted on you the way ducklings imprint on their mother, only your bond is psychic."

I blinked.

"Are you saying Bubbles thinks I'm her mom?"

Lois shrugged. "In a way. It would explain quite a few things about her behavior."

"I have never heard of a creature with the ability to bond in such a fashion, but I am in agreement with Lois," Buttercup said. "At the moment, it is the most logical explanation."

"Great." I glanced at Bubbles and somehow her innocent smile seemed a little broader, as if she understood. "Not only do we have to babysit a baby Viraquin, but now I have to worry about psychic parenting practices. How am I supposed to control what I'm thinking? What if she starts digging around into other things up there?" I pointed to my head. "I'm not exactly a model for child rearing. Being a bad example for pretty much everything is my motto."

"Pardon me for interrupting your self-pity, but I am detecting several incoming ships. It appears to be an entire armada."

The viewscreen switched to a rear-facing view and my jaw dropped as a virtual wall of spacecrafts closed on our position. They were gigantic cargo vessels with a small personnel area perched atop each enormous fuselage. Ships this large could exist nowhere but out in space and there were too many of them to count, all headed in our direction.

"Who is that?" My voice came out cracked and panicked.

"That would be the Dazbog gift armada, here to supply Dirk with the gifts for his Christmas deployment," Elliot said, not bothering to so much as glance at the incoming ships. "We, however, have no Dirk to carry out the mission."

"Incoming high priority transmission," Buttercup announced. "Shall I put them on screen?"

I looked at Lois, then back to Elliot. The little Dazbog made no move to join us, so I assumed first contact was up to the clueless humans. I set Bubbles on my chair and spun her around, so she faced the rear of the bridge, then stood with Lois at my side in front of the viewscreen.

"Go ahead and connect us," I said.

Almost before the words were out of my mouth, an image of a Dazbog clad in a red and white striped shirt and a green sport coat appeared. As if that fashion atrocity weren't enough, he didn't wear any pants, leaving the bright red fur on his legs exposed. He had a long white beard and a set of large, curved horns on his head. This Dazbog had years of wisdom under his belt, and I felt intimidated the moment he appeared on screen.

"The gift armada is on station and in place. Please notify Yule Ranger Dirk. We await his orders."

TWENTY-FOUR

"I am afraid Yule Ranger Dirk is indisposed at the moment." I wasn't quite sure what to say. I didn't want to tell him Dirk was down for the count, at least not yet. I needed a little time to come up with some sort of alternate plan. "Is there something we can do to help?"

"Negative. We haven't met the deployment requirements. I'm glad to see you made it, but I have not detected the Void Prism transport. Without that, we have no mission at all."

I held up a finger, finally able to give the Dazbog some good news. "That won't be necessary. I am Ben by the way. This is Lois. What should we call you?"

"I am Commander Dreg of the Dazbog Supply Fleet. I received word that two humans would be transporting Dirk to the deployment site. I confess I didn't believe it until I saw you with my own eyes."

"Well, I'm glad we could help."

I scanned the bridge, spinning around like a lunatic, realizing I had completely lost track of the Snow Globe.

"It's in my purse." Lois pointed toward her chair. "Dirk had it when ..."

She caught herself before she finished, casting a glance toward Commander Dreg on the screen. "I put it in my purse for safe keeping."

She hurried over and dug into the endless depths of her bright red bag and came up with the precious prism. She held it in the air with a smile and marched it back to me, carrying it as if it were an academy award.

"We have the required Void Prism." I took it from Lois and lifted it toward the screen for Commander Dreg to examine.

"Stand by for Void Prism verification. Do not move."

I stood with my arm outstretched while Commander Dreg accessed some controls off screen. Light from another display lit his face and he stood motionless as a scanner did its work right through our communication feed.

Seconds passed and my arm began to tire. Still, Commander Dreg didn't move, and I began to wonder if something had gone wrong.

"Did the transmission freeze?" Lois squinted at the screen, no doubt thinking the same thing. "Buttercup, can you reconnect?"

"The channel is open," Buttercup responded. "There is no need to reestablish communications."

I relaxed and lowered the Snow Globe to my chest, no longer able to hold it aloft. "Well, why isn't he saying anyth—"

"Void Prism scan complete." Commander Dreg reanimated, turning his gaze to us as if someone had flipped a switch to turn him back on. "Processing."

Commander Dreg turned and sped off screen, leaving us to stare at a very industrial background. Nothing but a utilitarian wall, steel railing and a bank of computer equipment. I might have been suspicious of the transmission freezing again except for the ever-flashing lights on the electronics array.

The tension grew as we waited in an uncomfortable silence. After what seemed like an eternity, I turned toward Elliot who sat on the floor, dutifully watching over his friend. "Is this, you know, normal?"

Elliot nodded his head without looking up. "It's just a formality. They have to scan the prism for imperfections. A damaged prism, well ... you wouldn't want to be the one standing in the fragmentation zone."

"Ben." Lois tugged at my sleeve, and I turned toward the screen to see Commander Dreg had returned.

"A fracture has been detected." His voice was firm and resolute. "The prism is unsuitable for deployment."

"What?" I started to lift the Snow Globe into the light to take a better look, when Elliot snatched it out of my hand. I didn't think anything would tear him away from Dirk's side, but apparently this was enough to shake him.

"That's impossible." Elliot had some sort of handheld optic. Something like a jeweler's lens but with more focus wheels and adjustments. He held the lens to his eye and peered into the globe, turning the prism in the light. He had only rotated it about a quarter of the way around before he let his arms fall to his sides, holding the implements in each hand.

"Commander Dreg is right. It's cracked, and not just a little. There is no way we can use this. It's a miracle we weren't all killed. If it were fractured any more Unicorns would have been the least of our worries."

Elliot inched his way over to Dirks chair and placed the Void Prism in the seat as if it were a case of nitroglycerin.

I shook my head in disbelief. "That's impossible. We risked everything to get that globe. How can it be—"

"When you tossed Dirk the Prism." Lois' voice sounded solemn and sad. "In the mine, when you had to use your revolver. It slipped through his hands and fell. There was no surface damage, but we didn't have time to check it any better."

I stared at her, my mouth half agape. I wanted to scream at her. Scream at someone, but it was no one's fault. Least of all hers. We were lucky to escape the Unicorns with our lives. No one had time to do an in-depth examination of the prism. Even if we did, going back to pick up another was out of the question.

My shoulders fell in utter defeat. How could we have come so far only to fail now?

Laughter pulled my attention to the Cur's chair, and I turned a furious glare in her direction. I promised no harm would come to her, but right now her laughter made me regret those words.

The Cur spun her chair to face the screen and Commander Dreg's eyes flashed with alarm.

"You have a Cur on your ship? This mission is compromised. Where is Dirk? I demand to speak to him."

"I'm afraid that's impossible at the moment."

Commander Dreg started to say something else, but I turned away from the screen to glare daggers at Oola.

"I apologize," she said. "It is not my intention to make light of your situation."

"Sure doesn't seem that way," Lois snapped, growling out the words in her danger voice. Apparently even her diplomacy had its limits.

"Do you have any idea what's at stake on that planet?" I said. "Our planet?"

Oola lost her smile and she nodded. "I understand it will disrupt your process and revert the planet to its normal state. An expensive sacrifice but a good first step in correcting the damage the Dazbog have done."

"Expensive?" I bared my teeth in a snarl. "Is that what you call the deaths of every child on the planet? Millions of innocent lives will be lost if we can't complete this mission, and you're giggling about it."

Oola wasn't laughing any longer. In fact, her eyes went wide with stunned horror. "Our intelligence sources reported the children's fatalities as propaganda."

"Propaganda?" Elliot clenched his fists but didn't make any move to charge toward her. "Why would anyone make up a horrible lie like that? Any of us can show you why stopping the process is fatal. All you had to do was ask. But all the Cur cares about is hoarding their precious prisms. Now children will die ... because of you. So go ahead and keep laughing."

Oola turned her head away, no longer meeting our eyes. "I'm sorry." Her words were barely a whisper, but they were only words. It would do nothing to save the children on our planet.

"All onboard LF units have programming set for emergency deployment in the event of a catastrophic failure." Commander Dreg's voice finally broke the uncomfortable silence.

I turned around and looked at his image on the screen. "Will that work?"

"The number of deliveries accomplished by the Dazbog on Christmas Eve verges on the impossible," Buttercup answered. "There is no way a few LF units can accomplish the same task. If they could, they would have done it a long time ago."

"It doesn't matter." The edge in Elliot's voice had disappeared and he stared at the floor. "It's hours before the Christmas Eve deployment and we have no one to carry out the mission, even if we did have a prism."

"That's not true." Dirk coughed and wheezed out a heavy breath. "They have you."

TWENTY-FIVE

"Who was that?" Commander Dreg leaned into his camera as if it would help him see further into our bridge. "Was that Dirk? What do you mean you have no one to carry out the mission?"

Elliot rushed to Dirk's side along with Lois. I turned to the screen and stared at Commander Dreg, not quite sure what to say. He couldn't see Dirk lying on the floor, but he had heard too much already. I had no idea what the commander would do if he knew his star Santa was down for the count.

"Uh ... I think we're going to have to call you back." I offered him an apologetic smile. "Buttercup, cut the transmission."

"Don't you dare—" It was all he got out before the screen blinked away to a view of the supply armada. The sight was awe-inspiring and altogether intimidating. To think it took this many ships to carry the gifts needed for Christmas, and a single Yule Ranger could deliver them all in one night. Incredible.

I hurried to Lois and Elliot who knelt at Dirk's side. I didn't have to be near him to see that he wasn't doing well. His eyes were open, but he looked pale and clammy. Dirk didn't even try to sit up, and for someone like him, that was telling enough in itself.

"I'm so sorry." Elliot streamed out his sorrow as Lois patted Dirk's head with a damp cloth. "You were right. I should never have tried to change things. My inventions only get everyone hurt. I thought I could help, but I just made everything worse."

"Hey!" Dirk shouted the word with more fire than I would have thought possible. Elliot glanced up to catch his eyes, and much to my surprise, Dirk offered him a kind smile. "You are a Yule Ranger. Stop acting like a one-week washout. I was the one who was wrong. I pushed against you because I don't like change, but also because I feared you might find a way to make Rangers like me obsolete."

Elliot looked stunned. His mouth moved as if he wanted to say something, but no sound came out.

"Dazbog like me are relics," Dirk continued. "If we're going to keep moving forward, we need more Rangers like you. A Dazbog who thinks outside the box and comes up with new solutions when all hope seems lost. If ever there was a time for you to shine, it's right now. Are you up to the task?"

Elliot stared at him for a second, then said, "No."

He shook his head in fervent little motions as he squeaked out the single word. "I'm no hero. That's what you do. Besides, the device probably won't even work."

"Wait." Lois' eyes flicked from Elliot to me and back to him. "What device? What're you talking about?"

"It doesn't matter." Elliot continued his self-reprehension. "I can't do this. Someone else has to—"

"There is no one else." I snapped the words a little sharper than I meant to, but it cut Elliot off all the same. "I'm tired of everyone believing they aren't good enough or acting like someone else is terrible because they look different or have a different way of thinking. Everyone is different. Get over it and find a way to make things work. Dirk's way is no better or worse than your way and vice versa."

"Fine words." Oola chimed in from her place on Elliot's chair. We all turned to face her. All but Dirk who could not see her from his position. "So long as you are not one of the billions suffering out there in the universe. The Dazbog have nurtured that suffering for generations because they can't look outward toward the future and the consequences of their actions. Even here, you may save your children, but in doing so you strike another blow against all those out there who would suffer as a result."

Elliot took a breath to say something, but I held out my hand to stop him and took a step in Oola's direction. "You claim the Dazbog cannot look outward, but can you look inward? You accuse them of suffering, yet you are willing to deal it out without regard when it serves your purpose. How many would suffer if the Cur were to have their way right now? Millions? Billions? Trillions? More? You both have a point and neither of you are right at the same time. Can't you both find a way to look outward toward healing without destroying the here and now?"

Oola's eyes shifted to the floor, and even Elliot didn't have anything to say.

I waited, letting the silence pressure them, then Oola finally let out a long breath. "There may perhaps be a way, but neither the Dazbog nor the Cur would agree to it. In fact, I was imprisoned for simply suggesting the solution."

I blinked. "Well, that sounds like a promising start. For now, can we all agree to care for the planet in crisis?"

Oola sighed but nodded her affirmation.

"Okay, now what about your part, Elliot?" I turned to look at him and found Lois and Dirk staring at him too.

"How about it?" Dirk coughed out the words and winced. "Are you a Yule Ranger or not?"

Lois raised an eyebrow, as if that was all she should have to add.

I realized I had no idea what Elliot had up his sleeve, but if Dirk thought it might work, I was willing to give anything a try.

"All right." Elliot stood, straight and proud. "I may have a way to make this happen. Call the gift armada and give them a green light to prep for maximum dispersal. I'll need a little time to set up my device, but when it's ready, we won't have any time to waste."

TWENTY-SIX

I stood in front of the forward viewscreen with Twitch on my shoulder. My faithful companion had always come through for us when we needed him, and right now I was grateful to have him standing with me.

"You ready for this big guy?"

Twitch chittered and I took a deep breath. Lois and Elliot were in the cargo hold setting up the new equipment and Dirk had relocated to a more comfortable position in my quarters. The only one left to back me up on this call was Oola, the Cur who would like nothing more than to see this all fail.

"Go ahead and open a channel, Buttercup."

"Commander Dreg's hails have grown increasingly more aggressive. He may be less than receptive to your call."

"Great." I sighed. "Go ahead and put him through."

The screen blinked to a view of Commander Dreg standing a little too close to the camera. He was already yelling when the transmission connected.

" ... dare you cut me off. I am the commander of the Dazbog

supply armada. I don't care what world you're from, I will have you strung up and ..."

He went on like that for a full three minutes before he ran out of breath and stopped shouting long enough for me to get a word in.

"Please accept my apology, Commander Dreg. I never intended to disrespect you or your station. An emergency situation caused us to neglect your hails. I contacted you as soon as I was able."

"Emergency situation?" Commander Dreg panted from his tirade. "What emergency situation?"

I resisted the urge to grin when he took the bait.

"I'm afraid I have a number of issues to brief you on. The first of which is a possible solution to the Void Prism."

That piqued Commander Dreg's attention and he backed off the camera to a more reasonable distance. "Do you have a second prism? It will have to be scanned for flaws as well and if—"

I held out a hand to interrupt him. "We don't have another prism, but we do have a Dazbog named Elliot. He claims to have a device that can do the same job."

"Elliot?" Commander Dreg shouted the name in obvious disbelief. "There is no replacement for the Void Prism. Elliot is going to get Dirk killed. I can't believe he would agree to any of this. I demand you bring Dirk to the bridge. If you fail to comply, I will board your vessel by force and take command of the operation."

I wasn't sure if he could do that, but I was sure Buttercup would give him more of a fight than he bargained for if he tried.

"Taking such brash action would only cause the mission to fail. As I understand it, you're needed on your ship to orchestrate the dispersal."

Commander Dreg sneered at the screen. "Don't tell me how to do my job. I am well aware of what's required. All you have produced are wild proposals and a Cur passenger. Produce Yule Ranger Dirk or I'll assume you're holding him captive against his will."

"He's not a captive, but I'm afraid he's in no shape to come to the bridge, or anywhere else for that matter. He was injured during our effort to obtain a Void Prism. He's stable and resting in my quarters, but he cannot fulfill the mission as planned."

Commander Dreg threw his arms into the air in exasperation. "No prism and no Yule Ranger. This mission is in a state of catastrophic failure. I'm initiating the LF unit protocol."

"Hold on," I said. "We have a replacement for the Void Prism, and we have a Yule Ranger. You and I both know the LF protocol won't come close to delivering all the packages on time. The least you can do is give this a shot. Elliot may not be the traditional type of Yule Ranger, but you don't need traditional right now. You need something different, and he's offering to provide it."

Commander Dreg paced in little circles pounding his forehead with the side of his fist. "I'm going to lose my commission over this. How long will it take for Ranger Elliot to prepare his device?"

"They're working on it right now. I'll notify you the moment they're ready."

"All right." Commander Dreg stopped pacing and leaned into the camera. "I will give him one chance. If his device fails, or if he isn't able to come through, I pull the plug and revert to the LF protocol. It may only deliver a fraction of the packages, but some is better than none at all."

I nodded. On that we did agree.

"Notify me the moment you're ready. I'll have the LF units on standby for dispersal."

"I will." I raised a finger to catch him before he ended the transmission. "There is one more tiny thing."

"Why do I feel like tiny to you is going to mean monumental to me?"

I turned to motion Oola forward. She stood with visible effort, holding her side as she walked, but she made her way to the front of the bridge where she could be seen on screen.

"What is this?" Commander Dreg's fury returned, but I held out a hand to stay his anger.

"I realize this is a bit unorthodox. This is Oola Targreth. She has some ideas she'd like to explore, but they require the knowledge and experience of a Dazbog like yourself."

"I will not consort with the enemy. It's near treason that you even have her on your ship."

"What if it meant peace for both of your people? All she wants to do is talk, and we have some time while Elliot prepares to deploy. Isn't a possibility of peace worth the price of a single conversation?"

Commander Dreg bared his teeth and grumbled. "You make big promises for a human. I will talk. Just make sure Elliot is ready to do his part in time to save Christmas."

TWENTY-SEVEN

"Come on." Lois and I stood side by side in the cargo hold, waiting for Elliot. He had ducked behind a stack of crates to change and now refused to come out. "The Santa uniform can't be that bad."

Bubbles had snuggled into a pile of netting with Twitch to take a nap and Oola was on the command deck having a very long conversation with Commander Dreg. There was a lot of yelling at first and I wondered if they would manage any productive discussion at all, but after a while they seemed to settle down to a more civil tone. Whatever they talked about, it had taken the better part of an hour. Plenty of time for Elliot to assemble his apparatus and don his new outfit.

"No way," Elliot called from the far side of the crates. "The deal is off. There's no way I'm wearing this thing."

I had no idea why he had ducked out of site to change in the first place. The Dazbog didn't even wear pants.

"At least come out and let us see," Lois urged. "We'll give you an honest opinion, I promise."

We waited another beat, then Elliot came sulking out from behind his crates, draped in his Santa suit.

Lois managed to cover her mouth, but I snorted out a laugh before I could cut it off.

"See, I told you." Elliot spun around to stalk behind the crates, but Lois hurried forward to pull him out again.

"It's not that bad," she lied.

The coat hung down to his knees and the shoulders draped over him like an oversized cape. It was like he'd been trapped under a fuzzy red parachute.

"Come on." Lois continued to tug on his arm. "Let's see what we can do with this thing." The patent leather belt hung loose around his waist, so Lois cinched it tight, then used the prong to poke a new hole so the buckle would fasten. She pulled a bit of the coat's fabric loose, so he didn't look quite so much like a hogtied marshmallow, then folded the cuffs to allow his hands to poke out of the sleeves. Elliot still held his Santa hat clenched in a fist, so Lois coaxed it free and perched it on his head. The hat promptly slid over his ears and eyes all the way to his nose.

"I have some safety pins in my purse." She lifted the hat and tilted it back, so it hung on his head more like a hood. "We can fix that too."

Elliot stared at me with a mix of disgust and frustration. "This is never going to work. A real Yule Ranger gets assaulted enough as it is, and he looks the part. Anyone who sees me is going to think the Grinch had a kid and he's back to steal Christmas a second time."

I laughed a little too hard at the joke, but it was a good excuse to relieve some of the pressure building behind my eyeballs.

"What do you know about the Grinch? You're a Dazbog.

Don't tell me Dr. Suess was one of yours." As I thought about it, Dr. Suess as an alien made a lot of sense.

"Naw." Elliot shook his head and had to catch his hat to keep it from falling off. "Popular Christmas folklore is required reading for any deployment. Dirk had been assigned to Earth, and I was ... am his apprentice."

"First of all," I said. "You have officially graduated past apprentice, and you are, and always have been, a real Yule Ranger. Just because you used brains instead of brawn doesn't mean you don't belong here. You're giving us our only hope of success."

I turned and motioned toward the apparatus he and Lois had assembled. "No one but you could have done this."

The main part of the contraption was no bigger than a large shoebox, but the clear casing revealed an intricate set of mirrors, crystals and electronics. The inner workings all looked to be made of brass, but something told me it was nothing so mundane. Outside the box, coiled wires led to twin cylindrical towers, between which the subject was meant to stand. The only other piece of equipment seemed to be a power cable far too dainty to energize a device of such magnitude. This was a piece of Dazbog technology designed to replace the indescribable power of the Void Prism, and somehow Elliot had built it small enough to disassemble and fit into his backpack.

"Right now, no one deserves to be here more than you." I clapped him on the shoulder. "If I had a way to help you, I would, but being Santa is a one Dazbog show."

Elliot jerked his head around to look at me. "It doesn't have to be."

I paused to clear my throat before tilting my ear in his direction. "How's that now?"

"We're breaking new ground here." Elliot smiled. "Why

not throw out the rule book all together? There's no reason my machine won't work for more than one. You could be my assistant."

"Now hold on."

"I think it's a wonderful idea." Lois grinned at us both as if she were a proud mother sending her children off to school. "I'm sure Elliot could use your help and imagine the experience of actually being Santa … well Santa's helper."

"I am not an elf," I snapped, but Elliot cut me off before I said any more.

"There's no reason you can't come too." Elliot beamed at the two of us. "With all three of us working together, I don't see how we can fail."

"But I need to say here and …" Lois hedged, then her shoulders slumped in defeat when she couldn't come up with a plausible excuse. "Fine. But if we're doing this, I get to choose the outfits."

TWENTY-EIGHT

To finish our preparations, we had to dock with Commander Dreg's flagship and transfer Elliot's apparatus to his launch area. I sent Lois and Elliot ahead with Dirk so they could drop him off at the medical bay to be cared for by the Dazbog. Oola rested comfortably, confined within my personal quarters. I tried to see the good in everyone, but Oola was still a wild card, and I wasn't quite ready to leave her all alone on the bridge while we were gone. Buttercup could defend herself, probably better than anyone else, but I figured confining Oola to my quarters had been a good compromise, and she needed the rest anyway.

As for me, I had a very important task to undertake. One that would require complete focus and attention. Once everyone was gone, I walked to the bridge and set Bubbles down on my chair. Twitch glided in next to her, but I kept my eyes focused on our baby Viraquin.

"Buttercup, do you monitor Bubbles' bioluminescence for any sign of communication? I mean, has she ever really tried to talk? I remember there was that one instance when she said thank you after we rescued her from that slave trader, but other than that, have you noticed anything?"

"Negative. I monitor all visual activity on the bridge and while you are away. I would tell you if she had attempted communication."

I sighed and stared into Bubbles' eyes. Lois was right, at least part way. I didn't agree with punishing Bubbles every time she folded, but we did need to set boundaries somehow. And I needed to find a way to do it now. I was about to split into countless copies of myself and travel all over the Earth. I couldn't have Bubbles trying to fold in on every single one of them. I didn't even know what that would look like. I was just sure it wouldn't be good. I had to find a way to make her understand. She had to stay here.

"Bubbles," I started. "I'm going on an important mission, and you can't come with me. It will be very dangerous for you."

I nodded and Bubbles gurgled and smiled, inching forward to hop into my arms.

"No." I pushed her gently into the chair. "You have to stay here."

Bubbles pouted then inched forward, but I persisted, shaking my head. "No. It's dangerous."

Bubbles growled out a little noise then folded right before my eyes. She popped out above my head and I had to catch her to keep her from falling. She cooed and giggled, but rather than hold her, I sat her down on the chair again.

"This isn't working."

Bubbles growled with frustration again, and I scratched my head trying to come up with another idea, then she did something that I didn't expect. Her bioluminescence altered to a pattern I recognized as communication ... at least I thought it did. "Buttercup did she just ..."

"Yes." She sounded almost as astounded as me. "She said, 'Ben stay.'"

"What? She knows my name?" I felt an odd mixture of proud parent and confused frustration that she hadn't communicated with us before.

"I have an idea." I spun Bubbles around to face the main viewscreen. "Can you emulate her light patterns on your screen in a way that she might recognize?"

"I can try. What would you like me to say?"

"Promise be back soon. Too dangerous for Bubbles."

"Are you sure? That is quite a bit for a first time."

"It's worth a shot. At least we'll know where we stand."

Buttercup flashed a beautiful array of blue light across her screen and Bubbles watched with intensity, her face darkening more with every moment.

As soon as Buttercup was done, Bubbles began to flash a patterned response.

"You little stinker. All this time we thought we had no way to communicate and here you are, chatting up a storm. What did she say?"

"Bubbles not stay. Go with."

I crouched in front of her and placed a tender hand on her head. I peered into her eyes not with anger or frustration, but with empathy and understanding.

"Tell her this. Ben keep Bubbles safe. Ben loves Bubbles. Keep Bubbles from being hurt. Stay with Twitch. Promise to be back soon."

Buttercup complied and I watched Bubbles the entire time, hoping my love and concern for her wellbeing would come through.

This time she did not appear angry. She looked sad and

maybe a little worried, but she flashed a short response, and that was it.

"Well? What did she say?"

"Just one word, yes."

I wanted to laugh. I was so happy. I couldn't believe we finally had a way to communicate. I rubbed her head and smiled at her. For now, this would have to be enough. I had to go, and I didn't want to wait any longer for Bubbles to change her mind.

"Twitch, you're in charge." I and gave him a little fist bump. "You watch over things here till I come back."

"What am I, a bucket of bolts?" Buttercup chided.

"You know what I mean. Can you tell Bubbles, thank you?"

Buttercup flashed the words on her screen and Bubbles responded.

"She said, love Ben too, come back soon."

TWENTY-NINE

Commander Dreg's launch area was not what I expected. I thought it would look like a cargo bay or a flight deck, but the place resembled something closer to a Star Trek transporter room. The walls were spotless and white, rising to recessed lighting on the ceiling. The floor was covered in polished red tile, but the real curiosity was the round platform in the center of the room. It reminded me of glossy obsidian and if I didn't know better, I would have said it was a miniature stage. Considering the way Elliot worked to affix his apparatus behind it, I had to assume it played a pivotal part in our mission. It was also the only visible reason for us to be here ... almost.

"Commander Dreg let you borrow one of his sport coats?" Lois laughed as I strolled into the room. "Red velvet suits you."

"Yeah, the mint green shirt and red and white striped tie really pulls it all together. I guess I should be thankful the Dazbog don't wear pants. At least I can wear my jeans."

"Yes. The jeans are a nice touch."

"What about you? How did you luck out with the nice outfit?"

Lois smoothed her green velvet dress and adjusted the fluffy white hem at the bottom. "Commander Dreg said he pulled it from the gift stores. He was going to find one for you too, but I told him it wasn't your color."

I narrowed my eyes at her. "Very funny. Notice anything else about my outfit?"

Lois appraised me one more time, then her jaw dropped. "Where is Bubbles?"

"You're not going to believe this, but that little stinker has been holding out on us this whole time. She can talk!"

"What?!" She stamped her foot. "And I wasn't there to see it?"

"Don't worry, she has plenty to say. We just had to figure out how to get her to say it. Buttercup used the light-form language to explain the danger here and she agreed to stay back."

Lois put her hand on her hips and nodded. "Well look at you, all proud parent of the year."

"I still don't agree with the whole punishment idea, but you were right. We needed to set boundaries. Maybe we can work together and figure out a good way forward after this."

"I think that's a great idea," Lois said. "And thank you for admitting I was right."

I opened my mouth to say that wasn't quite what I meant, but Elliot cut me off.

"If you two are done patting yourselves on the back, can one of you help me?" He struggled to line up one of his towering uprights without pulling his apparatus box onto the floor.

I hurried over and adjusted the pedestal that held the box

just before the whole thing toppled over. Elliot's apparatus box was much larger than the Void Prism, so it made the pedestal a little top heavy and dangerous.

"Are you sure we shouldn't find something else to set this on?"

Elliot shook his head and fumbled with something on the rear of the pedestal as I stepped away. Then he stepped back and gave it a hard kick.

My heart lurched to a halt and Lois let out an involuntary scream, but Elliot only smiled. "Electromagnetic seating. It secures everything to the floor. A Void Prism would be just as dangerous if it fell over."

I let out a breath and resisted the urge to strangle him for scaring us half to death. "Maybe next time you could try telling us instead."

"And miss that reaction?" He laughed. "No way."

He turned and walked between the two upright posts and motioned to the suspect stage on the floor.

"This technology is one of the Dazbog's most closely held secrets. This is what will transport us to our destination and bring us back again."

"What do you mean?" Lois walked around the stage but didn't step on it.

"We call it the Backlash. It has its limitations, but this is the other half of the equation for delivering all the packages in one night."

"Are you telling me this is a transporter?" I scanned the room, hardly able to believe my eyes. I had been spot on in my assessment, and now I was going to travel Star Trek style down to the planet.

"Yes and no." Elliot handed us each a medallion and clipped one of his own inside his jacket. "Like I said, the Backlash has limitations. In very short distances, like from here to the supply ships, it can be used as a one-way transport, but when the distance is stretched further, there is a boomerang effect."

"Boomerang?" I said. "As in we'll snap back to where we started from?"

"Exactly. Keep that medallion on you at all times. It's a locator beacon in case something goes wrong. You will have one minute to make your delivery before the Backlash snaps you back to the supply ships to load up again."

"What do you mean if something goes wrong?" I said. "And how are we supposed to do everything in one minute?"

Elliot nodded. "There's a reason Yule Rangers are the elite. This is no walk in the park."

"How dangerous is this?" Lois stared at the equipment we were about to throw ourselves into. "Say on a scale of one to ten."

"Maybe a two."

"Two isn't bad." I grinned. "You couldn't ask for more than that."

"Wait." Eliot's brow furrowed in confusion. "Did you mean ten is the worst or is one as bad as it can get? I always mix them up."

"Ten is the worst," Lois said, but I already knew what Elliot's answer would be.

"Then it is definitely a nine. Oh, I forgot about the fact that none of us have done this before. Better make it a ten."

I groaned. "Please tell me you have at least tested this thing."

"When you say test, you mean ..."

"I mean, you have used your invention, and it worked."

"Not as much as you might hope. Not at all, actually. No

one ever allowed me to examine a Void Prism, so this apparatus is based on theory. I'm confident it will work though."

"I think we should raise the scale to eleven." Lois wrung her hands with nervous tension.

"Or maybe a fifteen," I countered. "I guess there's only one way for us to know for sure. What's the worst that can happen?"

I snapped my arm toward Elliot, who had some horrible explanation poised on his lips. "Do not answer that."

Elliot let a breath out and pressed his lips into a tight line instead.

"Good," I said. "Now power this bad boy up. It's Christmas Eve. Let's take this baby for a spin."

THIRTY

The three of us stood shoulder to shoulder on the Backlash Transporter, each of us shaking like a leaf. We had put our lives in the hands of this little Dazbog, and now we were about to see if those hands would drop us right into oblivion.

"How long does it take for this thing to warm up?" I kept my eyes forward according to Elliot's orders. He said staring at the apparatus when it fired off could be devastating to my eyesight. The fun little quirks kept on coming.

"I'm not sure how much longer I can stand here and remain in control of my bladder."

"Ben Roberts," Lois scolded. "I'm not going to spend an entire night delivering Christmas gifts with you smelling like pee."

"I powered everything on. If my calculations are correct, we should be feeling the pull right about—"

It was all I heard before something tugged at my midsection, then yanked me through a virtual space the size of a pencil. A second later, the space squirted me out, and we all stood in a booth the size of a walk-in closet, facing a green, cherub-faced LF unit bearing an armful of gifts.

"Did it work?" I turned my head to the left to check on Elliot. Then a quick glance to the right drew a very unmanly scream from my throat. I pointed at Lois' head and, much to my dismay, she pointed at mine as well.

"Your hair is purple." Not just purple, but a vibrant shade of violet that bordered on fluorescent.

"So is yours."

We both turned to a very perplexed-looking Elliot.

"I guess I forgot to recalibrate a few settings on the apparatus to allow for human biology, sorry. I'll have to fix that."

"Fix that!" I shook with frustration. "What if it had turned our skin purple, or worse?"

"I said I was sorry."

I clenched my fists to try and calm my nerves. There was no time to worry about this now, at least we were in one piece. We could discuss our creative color additions later.

"Did the apparatus work?" My voice came out much calmer than I felt. "Why are we standing in a booth?"

"The booth is here to prevent us from seeing thousands of our split selves and getting distracted. I can only assume it worked because if it didn't, we would have been vaporized to atoms."

I took a breath and turned toward Lois. "Can you talk to him? I can't do it anymore."

Lois put a calming hand on my shoulder and looked at Elliot. "You might have mentioned the atomizer possibility earlier."

"He told me not to say anything." Elliot's voice had risen about three octaves. "When he asked what's the worst that could happen, he said he didn't want to know."

Lois snorted a little laugh and peered at me. "He's not wrong."

"Look," Elliot said. "I don't mean to be insensitive, but we have a job to do and saying we have limited time is an understatement. It's Christmas Eve, and we are already five minutes behind schedule."

Elliot turned toward the LF unit and took the elaborately wrapped gifts out of its arms. When the LF unit clacked away and returned on its spidery legs with more packages Elliot nodded for us to do the same. I took my share, but my mind wasn't on the job. I couldn't fathom that there were countless versions of me out there right now. I didn't feel any different. I felt like me. Did all the other copies feel the same? Then I wondered if I was a copy. My head began to spin with the implications.

My thoughts were cut off when the Backlash sucked the three of us backward, packages and all, then slammed us down in a large apartment decorated in lights and garland. A huge tree stood over piles of gifts in the corner and the sense of Christmas spirit allayed my distress. Just like that, we were back on Earth. I had almost forgotten how good it felt to be home.

I stood with Lois looking around the room, packages in hand, staring in absolute wonder. Had we really stepped into the boots of Santa Claus? I could hardly believe we were the ones who would save Christmas.

"Come on." Elliot whispered. He had already placed his gifts under the tree. "We only have a few seconds. You need to hurry."

Lois and I rushed toward the tree, and I set my packages on the ground. My grin was ear to ear when I turned and found myself face-to-face with a one-hundred-and twenty-pound

Rottweiler. He showed his teeth too, but I didn't think he was grinning. I stooped there, frozen with fear, then the dog launched itself at my face ... just as the Backlash fulfilled its namesake and pulled me back through the pencil pathway to our gift booth.

"One down," Elliot looked absolutely giddy. I on the other hand still crouched near the floor, trembling in fear. "Only one thousand four hundred and thirty-nine to go."

THIRTY-ONE

We continued gift giving and joy spreading for almost nineteen hours. Lois and I were exhausted. We had breaks here and there. When a time zone passed over the ocean, for instance, but then we made up for it when we hit population-dense areas like Tokyo or Dubai. The LF units provided ultra-high energy snacks that were suspect in their effectiveness, to say the least. Hour after hour we kept going. The whole thing felt oddly satisfying in an overly organized, Para-militaristic sort of way. Yes, we had saved the children, but it was more than that. We were accomplishing the impossible so families all over the world could wake up and experience the magic of Christmas. It was no small thing, and I felt humbled to be a part of it.

The Backlash delivery window did have quite a few drawbacks. Stockings were the worst. Stuffing those things full of candy and toys in under a minute was near to impossible. Lois took over the job after I exploded two back-to-back jumbo bags of M&Ms. Those bags never seemed to hold a lot of candy until a million of those colorful little nuggets rattled all over the floor.

The cookies and milk were interesting too. Turns out Lois was lactose intolerant and Elliot couldn't have sugar. Something about messing with his ADHD. About halfway through our first time zone, I finally had to resort to breaking the cookies in half and pouring the milk in the sink. Elliot said that was a smarter choice anyway. I guess slipping Santa a roofie is a thing. Someone needed to update the naughty list and those people should be on it.

Back on the supply ship, the three of us loaded up with a small delivery and prepped for our next drop. By now, the Backlash experience was nothing special. I had gotten used to the whole, sucked through a straw sensation, but when we landed for this next stop, my breath caught in my throat.

"Isn't this ..." Lois looked at me.

"It's the Buzzard's Roost." I nodded. The place hadn't changed one bit. The red and black tile floor, the pool table in the back, the corrugated steel bar where Isaac poured out his drinks and wisdom. I spent a lot of time in this place; eating, drinking, talking. It represented a big part of my old life. The one I gave up the moment Buttercup came crashing down to Earth. From that point on, everything changed. Aliens were real, evil A.I.s became the enemy and, of course, I met Lois. I couldn't do any of this without her. I missed this old town, but I wouldn't trade any of it for my life in the stars. I had seen too many things, been to too many places, and we were just getting started.

I set my packages next to a little tree on the bar and hurried around the counter.

"What are you doing?" Lois watched me along with Elliot. There wasn't much to do on this run, so they were already waiting for the Backlash to yank us back again.

"Hold on a sec."

I grabbed a highball glass and my favorite scotch. Highland Park. Isaac always kept it in stock just for me. I poured a glass, then snatched a napkin out of the bin. I wrote as fast as I could. I knew I only had seconds, but I wanted to leave Isaac something special. He had always been there for me, and he deserved to know I was all right.

I finished scrawling the message, as the Backlash seized us. I was pretty sure I left the pen standing on end as we departed.

The message was simple. "Never stop chasing your aliens. You just might find them."

I had no doubt Isaac would know what it meant and who wrote it. We had more than one conversation on the subject, and he had never judged or belittled me. He just listened, like any good bartender would. And sometimes that's all you really need.

THIRTY-TWO

There were many things I forgot to ask before we embarked on our impossible Christmas mission. How would the Backlash feel, why do dogs hate Santa, or how did bathroom breaks work for a million clones? Turns out the most important question of all didn't come until the very end. What happens when it's all over?

I remember Elliot saying his apparatus worked on a timer. The Void Prisms had a finite duration as well. They both lasted precisely twenty-four hours. When the timer expired, the apparatus shut off and the countless copies lingering on the supply ships smashed back to the same spot where they started on the Dazbog flagship, leaving nothing but dust in their wake. One moment we were split, the next we weren't. Like walking out of the hall of mirrors in a fun house. Once you left, all the duplicate reflections were ... just gone.

Unlike a two-dimensional mirror, however, my copies all had separate memories and experiences from the last twenty-four hours and now all those memories were stuffed into my single, solitary head. My brain felt like a marshmallow in a microwave and I pressed my palms against my temples as if that might keep it from exploding.

Lois appeared to be having a similar experience as she had adopted the same pose. Her face had turned three shades of crimson and breathing seemed impossible for either of us. I had trouble thinking or seeing. If something didn't let up soon, we would both round out our mission by lying on the floor, curled in the fetal position.

"Stand back." I heard the voice as if in a dream. I squinted at the colorful figure charging in my direction and made a half-hearted attempt to defend myself, but I wasn't fit to fight off a goldfish.

The figure pressed something silver against my neck and I added sharp lancing pain to my list of ailments. Whatever the figure did infused fire into my veins, but within seconds, the pressure in my mind began to wane. The feeling of an impending memory detonation subsided, and I looked around to see Commander Dreg injecting something into Lois' neck with a chrome plated inoculation gun. She stiffened at the pain like I did, then I saw the relief wash over her face as well.

"Human brains were never meant to handle that kind of memory fusion." He leveled a glare at Elliot as if he should have been the one prepared for this.

Elliot rubbed the back of his neck and grimaced. "Yeah, I guess there were a few things that slipped past me, but overall, I would say this was a success."

"You mean besides almost melting our brains and turning our hair purple?" My head started to feel like my own again, though I had a very disturbing sense that all my split memories remained eager to break free. "Am I ever going to be able to walk into a barber shop again?"

"I don't know why a barber would refuse to cut purple hair, assuming it has the same density and tensile strength as—"

Lois hurried over to put a hand on Elliot's shoulder. "I'm sure it will be fine. I think it looks great. How many humans can say they have naturally violet hair?"

"You're not helping."

She grinned. "I think you're focusing on the wrong thing here. Elliot's apparatus worked. We saved Christmas, and now the Dazbog will never have to depend on the Cur for Void Prisms."

"I'm not so sure that's a good thing." I turned and was surprised to see Oola enter the transport room. Her walk seemed slow and deliberate, making it apparent that she still felt the effects of her injury. I was even more surprised when Commander Dreg walked over to offer his arm in support.

"After our conference, I thought it would be a nice gesture to invite Oola onto my ship. I contacted ... Buttercup?" Commander Dreg raised an eyebrow but didn't question it further. "She agreed to release Oola so she could visit. We had a long conversation and discovered some surprising things about each of our people."

Oola dipped her head in his direction and actually smiled. A far cry from the Cur who cowered in anger and fear less than two days ago. "Having this apparatus is a boon for the Dazbog, but the Cur will see it only as a limitless threat to all they hold dear."

"Oola and I have worked out a treaty that could be agreeable to both our species, but I am afraid it is too late to broker a peace between them."

"Why?" Lois sounded angry at Commander Dreg's defeatist attitude. "It's never too late to fight for peace. You can never stop trying. Look at the two of you. A few days ago, I bet neither of you would have imagined standing together on this ship, but here you are."

"Lois is right." I stepped off the platform toward the two would-be delegates. "Nothing is impossible. You just have to keep trying. The Dazbog and the Cur may not see eye to eye, but if you two can find a way to work things out, so can they."

Commander Dreg nodded but I didn't think it was because he had changed his mind. "If we had more time, it might be possible, but I received word from the advanced fleet. The Cur have broken through our lines and are headed for our planet. The Dazbog will have no choice but to defend themselves with devastating global defenses. With the Cur's access to Void Prisms, the clash between the two factions will likely mean the end of both our species."

Oola nodded in solemn agreement. "The Cur have poured everything into this assault. If the Cur fleet is destroyed, there will be nothing left. But I fear they will do enough damage to the Dazbog planet to ensure their destruction as well."

"This can't be happening." I ran my hands through my very purple hair. "We save Christmas on Earth only to learn it was all for nothing? I don't accept that."

I turned slightly and lifted my gaze to the ceiling. "Buttercup, can we make it to the Dazbog home world before the Cur?"

"Perhaps. The Cur are running under full power, but they are also engaged with several Dazbog ships. That combined with the logistics of moving such a large fleet could give us the time we need to beat them there."

"What are you thinking?" Lois looked at me. She would have heard Buttercup's response over our internal communications system but no one else would.

"If we could get you between the Cur and the Dazbog, do you think you could get them to listen?"

I had my eyes on Commander Dreg, but his gaze was locked on Oola.

"If you can place us in the path of the Cur and open a communications channel, I might be able to convince them to at least speak with us."

Elliot eyed her with suspicion. "Why were you on that planet with the Unicorns? You said something about being their captive. Do you have some kind of political connection we don't know about?"

I looked at Elliot, surprised that I hadn't made that connection myself, or at least questioned why she had been stuck on that planet.

Oola offered only a sad smile. "My political connections are complicated, and I was imprisoned because of my ideals. They are both concerns that could either help or hinder our cause."

"The Dazbog are stubborn," Commander Dreg said. "But I have been with the service for a long time. They may listen to me as well."

"Then it's settled." I turned to Lois, but she was already hurrying toward the airlock. She knew as well as I did there wasn't a second to lose. "Buttercup is the fastest ship here and we need to get you to the front line. We'll just have to hope both sides don't vaporize us when we get there."

THIRTY-THREE

"Do you even have a plan here?" Lois stood near me next to my captain's chair on the bridge. We traveled at maximum speed through the Warpstream and though we had outpaced the bulk of the Cur fleet, we still had no idea how to keep the two sides from destroying each other long enough to hear what Oola and Commander Dreg had to say.

I shook my head and glanced at Bubbles who sat gleefully in my arm. Once I returned to the ship, she was so happy to see me she folded right into my hands, and I hadn't been able to put her down since. I counted the little victories. We could now communicate, and Bubbles had kept her word. We had taken our first step toward acceptable space folding behavior and that was a win.

"I know this isn't a great plan, but I'm pressing forward with the hope that a solution will present itself once we get there." That wasn't what Lois wanted to hear, but I owed her the truth. How could you even plan a single pirate-ship blockade between two warring superpowers? Improvising seemed like our best option. Good thing it was my specialty.

Oola stood at the rear of the bridge talking to Commander Dreg and Elliot. Dirk was with the supply fleet being treated, and reports said he was stable and improving. I tried to get Elliot to stay behind as well, but he wouldn't have it. He said we had risked our lives to help him, and he was not about to let us go into this thing without doing the same, even if it meant standing behind us for moral support. Elliot might be the smallest Dazbog I'd ever met, but he was also the strongest.

"Dropping out of Warpstream now," Buttercup announced. "I am reading several Cur ships just out of range of the Dazbog planetary defenses. There appears to be a command ship and an escort contingency."

"They are waiting for the rest of the fleet to arrive so they can move in and attack in force," Oola said. "We don't have much time."

Buttercup dropped out of warp between the Cur ships and Daedala, the Dazbog planet. We didn't have time for subtlety or to ease our way in hoping they would stand down. I wanted to make a statement, small as Buttercup may be, and there was little doubt that we had been noticed.

"I am reading multiple missile locks on our position," Buttercup said.

"From where?" I contemplated sitting in my chair but there was no point. We weren't here to fight.

"From everywhere," Buttercup answered. "Both Dazbog and Cur forces are preparing to fire."

"Open a channel, send it wide to anyone who will listen." I waited half a beat then, "We have delegates on board from both the Cur and Dazbog Factions. Do not fire."

We all held our breath. When we weren't rendered to slag, I sighed and ushered Oola and Commander Dreg forward. "It's now or never."

They moved to stand front and center before the main screen while Lois and I stood off to the side with Elliot.

"Hold on one second." I sat Bubbles on Lois' chair and scanned the bridge for Twitch. He glided in from behind me and landed on my shoulder, then ran down to join Bubbles. "You two be good. This is important, and we can't afford interruptions."

I leveled my gaze at Bubbles, and she pouted a bit, but she got the message, so I spun the chair away and faced the screen.

"Okay. Open the video feed. Let them see who we have standing here."

It was the Cur who responded first.

"Oola. What are you doing there? How did you get out of the Void Prism mines? You were to stay there until we settled this."

The Cur on the screen had features similar to Oola, but he was somewhat larger and much more muscular. He wore Beige robes like Oola and shared her haunting white eyes, but his expression came across as anything but pleased.

"Father, this is the commander of the Dazbog supply fleet and one of their highest-ranking officers, Commander Dreg."

Lois and I blinked at each other. Father? Oola had been holding out on us. And what kind of father imprisons his daughter on a wasteland planet with a bunch of savage Unicorns?

"Commander Dreg, this is my father, Chalock Zorah, Cur High Magnate."

"Zorah?" I whispered, noticing he had a different last name than Oola.

"Maybe it is her mother's name." Lois shrugged.

"We are here to request an audience between you and

Dazbog command," Oola continued. "You must see that this course will only lead to our mutual destruction."

The Dazbog had not yet joined the party. I had no doubt they were listening, but we needed them to be more than passive participants.

"This is Commander Dreg of the Dazbog fleet. The Cur has been kind enough to respond. Is the Dazbog so rude as to ignore our call?"

Still, no answer.

"Buttercup," I whispered under my breath. "Scan the area. Are you picking up any Arges class ships?"

Lois raised an eyebrow at me, but I kept my attention forward.

"Affirmative. There is one ship. The identifier has it registered as the Crooked Foot."

I almost cheered out loud. We knew that ship. We met the new captain on our last mission. He was a decorated ex-Yule Ranger and helped us more than once when we were in a bad situation.

"Hail that ship on a subchannel and see if you can get him to join this call."

Buttercup went quiet for a moment, then a familiar face popped up on the split screen. It was our friend Stella. Tough as nails and twice as salty. If diplomacy didn't work, maybe Stella could speak a language Dazbog command would understand.

"Now, why did you go dragging me into this mess? I was perfectly happy, taking orders and fighting the Cur."

"Something tells me you have never been much for taking orders." I took a step forward to move into the camera.

"Father, this is Captain Ben Roberts. We are also joined by his first officer, Lois Garraway and Yule Ranger Elliot."

The Cur High Magnate crossed his arms. "You have sixty seconds before I close this channel and blow that mechanized planet out of orbit."

"Easy." I held up my hand. "We're hoping for peaceful talks here."

"Peaceful?" Stella laughed. "If it's peace you want, you're parked in the wrong solar system. For a couple of Vistics, you two sure find your fair share of trouble."

I nodded. "It's great to see you, Stella. I hoped you might put in a good word for us with Dazbog command."

"Put in a good word? My word is worth a pound of rat spit, but I will say this. The day the Cur is brave enough to show up when the Dazbog isn't? Well, on that day I would be embarrassed to call myself Dazbog. We're all out here watching, and a leader is only as good as those behind him. I'm not sure how many Dazbog would be willing to fight for a leader who would shy from a simple ..."

Stella's image disappeared and another familiar face took its place. One very red, very furious looking General Pen.

"I am Peloren Kreasha, high general of the Dazbog and no coward to the Cur."

"All right then." I clasped my hands together. "I suppose the gang's all here. We are asking for an audience hoping to prevent the mutual destruction of both your species. Considering the stakes involved, I don't think a few moments is too much to ask."

I stared at the screen and when neither of them answered, I took it as an invitation to continue.

"Oola Targreth and Commander Dreg have negotiated a—"

"They have no authority to negotiate anything!" General Pen shouted.

At the same time, Chalock, the Cur High Magnate yelled,

"I do not recognize the authority of Commander Dreg or anyone else for that matter!"

"Silence!" I held up my hands, shocked by the weight I had put behind my voice. I was even more surprised when they listened.

"You are both on the verge of exterminating your entire civilizations. All because you both believe your viewpoint is right. Let me tell you something. You're both right ... and wrong. Neither of you has all the answers, but if you would just realize you don't have to annihilate one another over a difference of opinion, you might find the other side can fill in some of those gaps. Just because you don't agree doesn't make you enemies. Listen to what these two have to say. After that, if you still want to burn the galaxy down around your ears, go ahead ... let us get out of the way first, but then ... go ahead and blast each other to bits."

Both the Cur High Magnate and the Dazbog General appeared stoic and unmoving, but at least they listened and that was a start.

"Would you like to begin?" Commander Dreg stepped back giving Oola the floor.

Oola inclined her head and looked mostly at her father, though she addressed both the leaders.

"The Cur maintain that the Dazbog has abused their technology to enlighten borderline civilizations and advance them to the intellectual and evolutionary transcendence necessary to become a space-faring species."

I could see General Pen open his mouth to speak but Oola held up a hand. "I am not here to argue that point, Commander Dreg will address that concern later. I mention that only because it brings to light an issue, I believe the Cur are unaware of. There are one hundred and thirty-four planets undergoing the Dazbog's treatment to evolve. On each of those planets, millions of children receive treatments. I have just returned from the human's home world, one of the planets under the Dazbog's care. Our people attempted to withhold vital technologies that would make the Dazbog's annual treatment impossible and in doing so, we would have killed every child on that planet."

General Pen nodded with righteous satisfaction, but Chalock could not hide his shock and disbelief.

"It is not your fault, father. Our intelligence has always reported this fact to be a falsehood manufactured by the Dazbog, but I have examined detailed examples of the process myself. If we were to destroy the Dazbog or force them to cease all operations, we would in essence be responsible for the murder of trillions of innocent children throughout the galaxy. For our part, the Cur cannot allow this to occur."

"So, you propose we pull out and let the Dazbog continue." Chalock had regained his composure and crossed his arms in defiance. "I would die first."

"This is only half of our proposal." Commander Dreg stepped forward taking up the argument. "While the sudden cessation of current treatments may be impossible, future treatments can be regulated. The Dazbog have always had the best of intentions in assisting borderline civilizations, but the Dazbog does not consider the future implications of artificial transcendence. Through our good will, we have caused suffering and even created monsters. This can no longer stand. With the Cur's help, we will develop strict sanctions and standards that must be met before new treatments are initiated. We must look past the present, and into the future, to work together and continue helping borderline species when it is warranted and sustainable by the surrounding systems. This is our proposal. We stay the course to save the children, and work together for a better, more viable future."

Time passed for what seemed like a century, then Chalock spoke first. "I am proud of you, Daughter. It took a great deal of bravery to do what you just did."

"I am not alone, Father."

"No, you are not." Chalock took a breath and straightened. "I'm willing to discuss these terms if General Peloren Kreasha is willing to open negotiations."

All eyes went to General Pen. He still wore a pinched, angry expression, but I had learned that he just looked like that most of the time.

"Pull your fleet back, and I'll agree to negotiations," General Pen said. "I have no wish to cause bloodshed where it is not needed."

"Agreed."

Then, just like that, the screen went dark. Both sides ended their transmission and left us gawking out into space.

"Well, that was easy." I clapped my hands together. "Is there anything else we need to do? Maybe save the universe from a flesh-eating virus?"

"Thank you." Oola walked over and wrapped me in a hug. I did my best to avoid her injured side, then she moved to Lois and Elliot to do the same. I had a feeling a photo of a Cur hugging a Dazbog would be rarer than the Void Prisms.

"I'm not going to tell General Pen about my invention until both sides settle their treaty," Elliot said. "I don't want to freak everyone out when they've finally decided to start talking."

"That's probably a good idea. News that the Void Prisms are no longer necessary will shift the balance of power in a big way. Let them work on diplomacy first, then celebrate your invention later." I ran my hand through my purple hair.

"Plus, it gives you time to work out some of the bugs in your system."

There was only one other problem, and all eyes went to Commander Dreg.

"Don't worry about me." He held up his hands in defense. "After everything we went through, the last thing I would do is ruin it by spilling your secret. My lips are sealed."

Lois sighed. "I guess there's only one thing left to do."

We both looked at Bubbles. After all the trials and turmoil, it had all been for one reason. A lead to get this little infant home.

THIRTY-FOUR

After docking with the Cur flagship to deliver Oola to her father, we headed to Daedala's surface to take the rest of our passengers home ... and to collect on a debt. We were met with a rather large contingent of LF units on the landing pad, along with one angry-looking general.

Lois and I walked down Buttercup's ramp behind Elliot and Commander Dreg. I had Bubbles in my arm. General Pen had already seen her, so I didn't see the point in keeping her hidden, and Twitch rode on my shoulder. I figured if we were going to be read the riot act, we should all enjoy it together.

General Pen met the two returning Dazbog first, amidst a sea of creepy cherub faces and gleaming white eyes. I wondered if all those LF units had been converted to some sort of battle mode for the upcoming invasion. Then I wondered if they were still programmed that way.

After they said hello, Elliot and Commander Dreg stepped aside to allow Lois and I through to greet the General. I held my hand out to shake his, but General Pen stared at me with those angry eyes. I really hoped the LF units weren't battle bots.

A full ten seconds passed, which seemed like an eternity, then General Pen cracked a smile, slapped my hand aside and jerked me in for a big ol' man-style bear hug. I was so shocked I let out a fearful screech. I barely had time to lift Bubbles out of the way to keep her from getting crushed. Twitch growled his displeasure at the sudden intrusion, but General Pen ignored him and kept on squeezing. After a few moments of vice like constriction, he let me go and clapped me on the shoulder. "You did a fine thing up there. You and your crew."

General Pen turned to Lois and gave her a much gentler hug. Then he stood back and pointed to Twitch and Bubbles too. "I haven't forgotten you. I'm sure you both had a hand in the success as well."

Twitch growled again, but Bubbles cooed in appreciation and a pattern of light danced across her skin.

General Pen laughed and touched Bubbles on the head. "And it's a good thing you stayed put, little one. Sometimes, having the courage to hold your position is harder than fighting the battle itself."

I peered at Bubbles, then at Lois in astonishment.

"Hold on." Lois held out her hand to interrupt. "Can you understand her?"

"Of course." General Pen sounded almost indignant at the accusation. "Yule Rangers could hardly fulfill their duties without being fluent in multiple forms of communication. Bubbles said her part in the plan was to remain safe on the ship."

Lois crossed her arms and pouted. "How am I the only one who doesn't get to talk to her?"

I snorted out a laugh. "I have a feeling now that we know

she can talk, Bubbles will have plenty to say. We just need to learn her language."

General Pen looked a bit uncomfortable, then he glanced up at my head. "Eh ... what's with the hair? I mean, on you it looks lovely dear." He smiled at Lois, then turned back to me. "But you look like an escaped lunatic."

I spun my head toward Elliot. He shuffled on his feet making the equipment in his backpack rattle. Hard to believe what he had in there could change the face of everything they knew.

"Yeah, well we had a little trouble with the Backlash." I lied. "I guess there are a few corrections that need to be made before a human can use it again."

General Pen's face lost some of its mirth. "Indeed. You understand the Backlash is considered one of the Dazbog's highest state secrets."

"We do," Lois said. "And Elliot never told us a thing about how it worked. We were nothing but willing passengers."

"And you, Yule Ranger Elliot." General Pen turned to look at him. "It seems we have all underestimated your ability. Tackling the human world on your first deployment is quite a feat, even with a little help. We'll have to see about getting you a permanent assignment."

Elliot's face lit up so bright it almost glowed. "Thank you, Sir."

"Commander, you will be rewarded for your bravery as well, though I am not sure what would be befitting a Dazbog of your station."

"Your gratitude is enough sir." Commander Dreg winked. "That and perhaps a bottle of that Peeri ale you stow away in your office."

General Pen narrowed his eyes at the commander. "Done. We can discuss how you know it's there later."

When he turned to us, he was all smiles again. "And what about the two of you? Is there something within my power that I can provide?"

I cleared my throat and gave Bubbles a little jiggle. His eyes went to the giggling lightshow in my arm.

"Ah yes. We had an agreement, did we not?"

I nodded. "We did. Lois and I would very much like to deliver this little girl to her mother."

"It seems your list of good deeds grows ever longer." General Pen turned to an LF unit standing off to our left. "LF 462."

The cherub nightmare came to life in an instant and clacked forward on its spidery little legs.

"Transmit coordinates for system 7-Alpha-6-Zeta-1 to their ships computer."

The LF unit hesitated a moment, then beeped and clacked into position.

"Is that it?"

"I have received coordinates to an uncharted section of deep space," Buttercup answered. "I cannot confirm that this is the correct location, but they have provided us with coordinates."

"That's it," General Pen answered. He couldn't hear Buttercup's response, so he assumed I spoke to him.

"Thank you, General Pen. I hope your talks go well and you find allies where you once had enemies."

"A hero and a philosopher." The General chuckled. "You better get going before I enlist you to head up the negotiations."

"No," Lois grabbed my arm and started tugging me backward. "Thank you, but we need to get going."

I didn't resist. Much as I loathed the thought of having to ever part with Bubbles, we had a destination. Considering our propensity for finding trouble, it would be better if we got going sooner rather than later.

"Thank you again General. Give our regards to Dirk. Oh, and about that thing with Stella ..."

General Pen's eyes narrowed to slits. "Stella and I have a long history. He has always been a pain in my haunches, but he also knows me better than most. I'll make sure he is rewarded for his part in all of this. Maybe a little payback too."

I had no idea what sort of payback General Pen had in mind, but I didn't want to be around when it happened.

"Well, tell him thanks again from me. And I still owe him that drink, and a little more."

"Will do."

Lois pulled me a little harder toward Buttercup's gangplank and we walked up the ramp. Twitch glided off my shoulder and into the ship. With Bubbles in my arm, I watched the Dazbog disappear as the door closed. We had risked life and limb, stopped a war, and even saved Christmas. Now it was time to bring Bubbles home. The thought was bittersweet, but if the universe had anything to say about it, we would run into plenty of trouble before we got there.

Don't let your space adventure end here. Find out if Ben, Lois and Buttercup can find Bubbles' mother
Space Pirate Reunion

THANKS FOR READING!

💬 Loved the ride?
Tell the galaxy! Leaving a quick review for *Yuletide Space Ranger* helps other readers discover the madness—and means the universe to this author.

Love *Yuletide Space Ranger*? Don't drift away just yet! 🚀 Join the **C.G. Harris Legion** for insider access to sneak peeks of upcoming books, top-secret story intel, exclusive giveaways, and of course, Hula Harry's legendary Drink of the Week 🍹 (it's weird, wild, and probably neon).
👉 https://www.cgharris.net/legion-sign-up-page

Craving more chaos, aliens, and sarcastic AI? Find out what happens next to Ben, Lois, Twitch and Bubbles in ***Space Pirate Reunion***.

Ben and Lois are closer to reuniting Bubbles with her long-lost alien mother, but just because they're closer doesn't mean it's going to be easy. They must face off against an army of spiderbots, killer mushrooms, and a colossal cave monster the size of a '69 Buick ... and that's just the warm up!

Download the exclusive prequel novella, **Fugitive Star Voyage,** for free and discover how the madness began.

https://dl.bookfunnel.com/fh4fi73370

CRAVE ADVENTURE AND MAYHEM?
OPEN A C.G. HARRIS BOOK

Hell's worst government agency

Saving the galaxy was never the plan, but neither was stealing a starship.

An empire built on fear meets the one hero it never saw coming.

HULA HARRYS DEVILISH DRINKS
SINFUL SIPS FROM THE UNDERWORLD

Welcome to Hula Harry's, the only tiki bar in Hell bold enough to serve drinks that burn twice. Inside this wickedly funny cocktail book, you'll find real, mixable recipes inspired by the chaos, characters, and dark humor of The Judas Files.

These are full-throttle hellfire cocktails—The Brimstone Mary, The Dumpster Fire, and more—each crafted to ignite your taste buds and maybe your dignity. Every drink is a real-world recipe with an infernal twist, perfect for fans who like their cocktails strong and their fiction delightfully twisted.

So pull up a barstool, ignore the smoke seeping from the floorboards, and let Hula Harry mix you something unforgettable. Because in Hell's favorite bar, the drinks are real, the laughs are loud, and the hangovers are legendary.

THE C.G. HARRIS LEGION — RECRUITMENT BRIEFING

You made it to the end of the book.
You survived the chaos.
You're exactly the kind of reader we want in the **C.G. Harris Legion**.

Thousands have already joined this elite squad of readers....
now it's your turn.

WHAT YOU GET AS A LEGION RECRUIT

Exclusive intel — early chapters, secret files, bonus stories

Giveaways & prizes — only for Legion members

Hula Harry's Drink of the Week — dangerously delicious

First alerts on new releases, Kickstarters, and launches

No cost. No spam. Just fun, chaos, and insider access.

Proceed to the next page for further instructions.

TO ACCEPT YOUR MISSION:

Scan the code.
Join the chaos.

ABOUT C.G. HARRIS
CHUCK HARRELSON & KERRIE FLANAGAN

Hold onto your warp drives and wizard hats. Chuck Harrelson and Kerrie Flanagan are the award-winning coauthor team of C.G. Harris, responsible for some of the most thrilling escapades in the multiverse! Together they take readers on a devilishly daring dive into the hellish world of *THE JUDAS FILES*, a wild ride through young adult dystopia with *THE RAX*, and a space pirate adventure full of cosmic swashbuckling action in *THE VIRAQUIN VOYAGE*.

When they're not busy crafting the next great American novel or penning a haiku about the existential dread of Mondays, you can find them in the throes of what could only be described as a culinary Cold War, fiercely debating which is the superior pie—New York's big, floppy, fold-it-like-a-newspaper slice or Chicago's deep-dish cheese casserole with a crust.

To this day the debate remains unresolved. But in the heated exchange of doughy discourse, one thing becomes clear: when it comes to pizza, the only real winner is whoever gets the last slice.

Got a burning question? A wild theory? A brilliant plot twist we *absolutely* need to write? Reach out—we'd love to hear from you: **CGharrisAuthor@gmail.com**

Want in on exclusive stories, sneak peeks at upcoming chaos, and book deals that'll make your TBR list cry for mercy?

www.ingramcontent.com/pod-product-compliance
Lightning Source LLC
Chambersburg PA
CBHW071912220626
47052CB00002B/318

* 9 7 8 1 7 3 7 3 9 0 5 5 8 *